CRIME FICTION

CRIME FICTION

*UEA Postgraduate
Creative Writing Anthology
2018*

CONTENTS

IAN RANKIN
Foreword

In the autumn of 2016 I took up the role of UNESCO Visiting Professor at the University of East Anglia, which had recently launched an MA in Crime Fiction. Several factors led me to accept the invitation. Writing is a largely solitary vocation, and I thought it would be interesting to be around other writers. There was also the prestige attached to UEA's Creative Writing faculty, but perhaps most importantly I wanted to dig deeper into crime fiction as a genre, exploring its history, appeal, strengths and potential limitations. I set a reading list for students which included Dickens's *Bleak House* and Muriel Spark's *The Driver's Seat,* alongside the more usual suspects. The class then discussed those books, using the discussions as a means to investigate these areas of interest.

As I came to know all the students, I also learned something of their own reasons for choosing to write crime fiction. As a reader, I've always been drawn to crime (and the thriller) because I'm interested in large moral questions of good and evil. The best crime novels tell us something of ourselves and the world around us. Reading these books leads to an exploration – and deeper understanding – of social issues, political issues, culture and history. If I want to know about a nation, I will turn to its crime stories. They may even show me areas to avoid, or good places to eat and drink. They will certainly furnish me with information about the inhabitants and the problems they face in life. All of this, however, must be done in an entertaining fashion. Crime writers are not polemicists. During my time at UEA we discussed the Martin Beck detective novels written by Maj Sjowall and Per Wahloo, who wrote about Sweden from a Marxist perspective without ever being tendentious or hectoring. They produced ten sublime novels about a group of police officers operating in a changing society and facing new types of crime with the passing years.

I was fascinated by the breadth of range and approach in the students' writing. They based their stories in past and present, and in different world cultures. These were not inward-looking or solipsistic novels. Yes, they were about the human condition (as all novels are) but they were also expansive and exploratory. Crime fiction in the UK has come a long way from the country house drawing room or the confines of 221B Baker Street, and there is ceasing to be the critical snobbery that built seemingly impermeable walls between the crime novel and the literary novel. It was once said that Ginger Rogers did everything Fred Astaire did, only backwards and in heels. In similar fashion, crime does everything the literary novel does, but without longueurs and a corrosive sense of entitlement.

By the time I had finished my stint as Visiting Professor, I had probably learned more from the extraordinarily capable students than they had from me. It is a distinct pleasure to be able to share a flavour of their work with readers. Make no mistake, these are the stars of the future – and you're reading them here first.

LAURA JOYCE
Introduction

It has been a joy, a pleasure, and a privilege to watch these thirteen crime writers find their voices and their stories. Though these extracts make the writing look effortless, I know how fantastically hard they have each worked to fashion their stories, and how much effort they have each expended. I have worked with each of the writers over the two years of the course, and I am proud of each of them. Writing the Introduction is bittersweet for me, as I am leaving UEA this summer, and so this is my last act as a teacher on the Crime MA.

Some of the most inspiring aspects of this collection are the ingenuity, the variety, and the originality of the writers. No two books are remotely alike, and there are no formulaic novels in here. There are psychological thrillers, procedurals with a twist, historical crime fiction, and novels that transcend all subgeneric categories. These novels give us the perspective of villains and detectives, but also of suspects, victims, and those who blur the line between all of these. There are novels from the perspective of police officers, cyber security experts, probation officers, forensic linguists, geographical profilers, and forensic experts, professional and 'unprofessional' detectives, families out for vengeance, and vigilantes on the streets.

Dimitris Akrivos is telling a thrilling story of corruption and bullying at the heart of contemporary Greek institutions, as well as a tender family story against the thrilling backdrop of Greek politics and national unsettlement.

Denise Beardon has written a compelling thriller about technology and its disastrous application, touching on cyber security, stalking, hate crime, and the unseen people charged with solving these proliferating problems. These difficulties are closer to home than she thinks...

Bob Jones has created a fantastic otherworld. The quarry is at the heart of this deeply disturbing tale of a Welsh town where all is not what it seems. Gangsters, corrupt officials, and amnesiac protagonists people this book along with a most unexpected hero.

Femi Kayode has written a powerful, highly plotted thriller that opens with high stakes that only get higher. A dissertation on the post-colonial context of the setting of Nigeria, as well as a pacy and atmospheric thriller, this is a real achievement.

Roe Lane has given us a stunning premise. An investigation from beyond the grave, from a most unusual protagonist. An astonishingly assured and utterly original story. Tender, compassionate, and funny.

Natalie Marlow includes a beautifully reconstructed 1930s Birmingham where interwar unrest, fascism, class battles, amateur pornography and a generous sprinkling of cocaine and champagne set the stage for a thriller which switches between the back streets, canals, and stately homes.

Nicola Monaghan uses forensic science impeccably to weave together historical and contemporary versions of Nottingham, imprinted over an architecture of horror, in her superb work of Midlands noir.

Niamh O'Connor is a brilliant cartographer of crime; by turns acidly comic and tender, she tells a human story of obsession, horror, and shame, and the dangers of female adolescence.

Louise Sharland offers such original characters: street pastors, vigilantes, rapists, and drug dealers on both sides of the tracks in Plymouth. The probation system never seemed so glamorous! Secrets are finally revealed in the last act, the fervour and danger revealed.

Peter Sibley has created a hugely original detective in his group of 'unprofessionals' set in Geneva. This novel contains a corrupt crime family, a look inside the world of the 1 per cent, and at the contrasting lifestyles of those forced to make money however they can. Secret identities, star-crossed love, and gorgeous cycling sequences make this book an entertaining read.

Mark Wightman is a fine artist. The glittering details of this historical crime ensure that the plot never wavers, through the rich, gorgeous moments in the writing.

Matt Willis has written a fast-paced, exciting, thriller. A breathless tale of a honeymoon gone disastrously wrong, and a resolution that shows old and new traditions existing uneasily together in Brazil.

Freya Wolfe makes linguistic analysis thrilling and totally compelling. This novel is full of storytelling, each strand unravelling and revealing a darker truth. The dark side of Sheffield comes alive in this beautifully written story.

I could not be prouder of this cohort of crime writers who have taught me so much this last two years. I'll miss them very much. I am so excited to see each of the authors reach their full potential, and I can't wait to see what they do next.

This diverse anthology comprises the latest work from the 2018 cohort of crime fiction writers studying UEA's renowned Creative Writing MA.

Dimitris Akrivos was born and raised in Athens where he trained as a lawyer. He has a PhD in criminology and currently works in the UK academic sector. When not teaching or writing, you'll find him browsing his local bookshop for his next read. *The Aquarium* is his debut novel.

dimitriosakrivos@gmail.com

The Aquarium

This was Orestis' second time at the Spartacos group counselling sessions and most likely his last. In an almost out-of-body experience, he pictured himself grabbing the guy at the top of the circle – David something from the Fifth Infantry Brigade – by the collar, wrapping his fingers around his windpipe and squeezing. Doing something, anything to shut him up. Some people just loved being the centre of attention. David was now talking about cats and dogs, for Christ's sake.

'You know how cats stay still in the middle of the road, waiting for the car to turn them into pulp?' David mumbled, wiping the snot running down his nose with the back of his hand. Snotty David was of a rather short build, with ginger hair. His face and arms were covered in freckles and his bottom lip made a distracting twitch every time he spoke. No wonder he had become an easy target for the army camp's Goliaths. 'Dogs will see your car approaching and run to the other side,' he went on, 'but cats just stay there, indecisive about whether they want to cross the road or turn back, looking at you with their glaring eyes, helpless, paralysed by fear, waiting for the inevitable to happen. That's how I felt when I saw them. It's so strange talking about it. I never told a soul, not even my wife. Just hid the memory deep inside my head, pretending it never happened, you know?'

Tears soon started rolling down David's face. *Surprise, surprise.* Everyone around the circle was nodding with compassion, encouraging him to continue. *Please, David. Tell us more, David. It'll make you feel better, David.* What a waste of time! In all fairness, Orestis knew they meant well but could they really be that naïve? He was so angry at them for thinking a pat on the shoulder and a prolonged sympathetic 'Ooooooh' could stop you from waking up in the middle of the night drenched in sweat, screaming, shaking, staring into blank space, unboxing the shitty gift your most hated uncle has brought you, putting it back in the box and trying to find a new hiding spot for it, hoping that getting it out of your sight can make pretending it's not there easier. But it is. You know it is. And your disgusting uncle keeps finding it, bringing it back to you, asking you to open it again, taking pleasure in the way you are clenching your teeth, wearing your happy face and acting like everything is fine.

'Take your time, David. You're in a safe space. Whenever you are ready...' Marios said in a soft, barely audible voice, touching the guy's knee.

Please, David. Tell us more, David. It'll definitely make you feel so much better, David.

David opened and closed his mouth three times, making an attempt to find the right words but becoming more and more aware of his inability to do so. The incomprehensible sounds he was producing soon turned into a full-on sob.

You're still a soldier, dammit. Man up! Sobs won't get you anywhere.

'That's it, let them flow,' Marios added reassuringly, as if he'd read Orestis' mind, and handed David a tissue. 'We're all friends here.'

Orestis tightened his grip around the seat of his wooden chair.

David made a hissing sound as he blew his nose. 'The day before,' he started again, 'they had ordered me and the other new recruits to get inside our sleeping bags and crawl,' – he made quotation marks with his fingers – '"like the filthy worms that we were" chest-down from one end of the room to the other. Then, the next morning, I was at the shower block, my body aching all over, my neck so stiff I could hardly move it.' He massaged his nape, not without some theatricality.

Thank you, David, we got the point.

'Water was still running from the shower heads in the cubicles to my right and left. I thought others from my group were still there, but they were gone. "Hey, Einstein, don't use up all the hot water," I think I shouted, trying to be heard above the sound of the running showers. I thought the physics teacher I had come in the showers with was still in the next cubicle.'

Another torrent of tears.

'The water was ice cold, so I turned the shower off, shampoo still on my head and palms. And then there they were. The minute I saw the four naked gorillas blocking my way, dicks in hand, I knew I was fucked. "Sorry, love, were you lost looking for the ladies?" the tall one said with a smirk on his face. He was the leader of the pack. All four of them laughed. They were all senior officers, so I knew beforehand this was a lost battle. God, who am I kidding? There *was* no battle! I couldn't move, I felt so exposed. They could take me down in a second, I didn't stand a chance.'

David leaned forward, placing his elbows on his knees and burying his face in his hands. The bald, bearded man to his left slowly placed his hand on David's back with some hesitation, as if attempting to pet a wounded dog, not knowing if it would lick him or eat him alive.

Please, David. Tell us more, David. My patience is running low, David.

David kept talking, his face still hidden behind his hands, his voice muffled. 'I covered my genitals with my hands. They laughed again. Foam was rolling down my forehead, burning my eyes, blurring my vision. "Oooooooh, he's so shy! What a cutie!" the one with the acne scars said, faking a high-pitched feminine voice while glancing sideways at the tall guy for approval. They were just standing there, so unashamed, so proud of themselves. My eyes hurt but I made sure they were fixed on their faces. I didn't want them to catch me looking below their waists. "He's not shy. He's just embarrassed to have such a tiny little dick. Aren't you, *fish*?" the third one said and sucked his teeth. From day one that's all us new recruits were to our superiors in army slang. "Wake up, *fish*. Faster, *fish*. Did you shed your scales before coming in, *fish*?" You don't quite get it until you find yourself floundering like one. I didn't see who threw the punch, but I felt a sharp pain in my stomach. I slipped and fell to the floor, hitting my head on the tiles. I tried to get up but slipped again, which triggered another round of laughter. They grabbed my ankles and dragged me out of the cubicle. I stayed on the floor, terrified, thinking they were going to fuck me, one after the other. They didn't, so...' David uncovered his face, revealing a bitter smile. 'Lucky me, right? The warm liquid that hit my face caught me off guard. Then the warmth extended to my chest and thighs.'

Orestis closed his eyes and took a deep breath to suppress an urgent need to scream.

'"Is this hot enough for you, *fish*?" the tall guy said. They were pissing on me. Can you believe it? I made another attempt to get up but the fourth guy, who hadn't said a word, put his foot on my neck and held me down. The pressure on my throat made me choke, but this only gave them a new target for their aiming game and led to even more hysterical laughter. I could taste their piss on my tongue, the ammonia-like smell in my nostrils. It was in my eyes, my ears. I started retching. The guy holding me down moved his foot to my chest.'

David took a gulp from the bottle of water he had by his feet as if to wash away the foul taste of urine from his mouth. The bald guy sitting next to him now also had tears running down his cheeks and, from a quick look around, Orestis realised most people in the group did too. *What's wrong with me?* he asked himself, not for the first time. Everyone was moved by David's ordeal. Everyone but him – another quick look around – and perhaps the hooded man sitting four seats away who, from what Orestis could see from the corner of his eye, was peering indifferently out the window at the concrete chaos of modern Athens.

'"You liked your golden shower, bitch?" they asked me. They didn't even let me—'

Orestis felt the walls closing in on him. He pushed his chair backwards, causing a loud screech, breaking the circle. He stood up, turned around and burst out the door before anyone had the chance to stop him. He could hear the stir caused by his departure even after he'd left the room.

'That's not cool, man!' someone yelled as he entered the toilet.

He turned on the tap and splashed his face with cold water again and again until his jumper was soaking wet. He looked at his red, swollen eyes in the mirror and told himself it was time. The last time, one more time.

He entered the cubicle behind him and locked the door. He closed the lid of the toilet bowl and sat on it. He unbuckled his belt and pulled his jeans down to his ankles. A weird combination of anticipation and guilt made his heart beat faster. He found what he was looking for in his front pocket, threw away the wax paper it was wrapped in and stretched the skin of his inner thigh with his fingers. The razor blade penetrated the outer layer of his flesh, sending a stinging, then burning sensation first to his leg and in a few seconds to his entire body. He had learnt to do it properly now: to control himself and not cut too deep, so that the wounds would heal faster. As the blade moved vertically down his thigh like a ship sailing parallel to old, now faded, routes through a sea of red waves, a gush of images flooded Orestis' vision. He leaned his back against the wall and just laid there in his boxers as if in a trance, searching for answers on a toilet ceiling, blade in hand, blood dripping down his leg and onto the floor.

'Partying on your own?' a gruff, disembodied voice echoed across the room. A head appeared above the cubicle wall, making Orestis jerk, startled. The man in the hood was resting his head on his arms, observing him. The hood covered most of his face. All Orestis could see was the tip of a pointy nose and a pair of full, dehydrated lips surrounded by a thick, scruffy beard. *How long has he been there for?* Orestis wondered.

'Jesus!' he shouted, dropping the blade to the floor and jumping to his feet. He pulled up his trousers, feeling like a teenager who'd been caught masturbating. The sudden stretch of his thigh muscle triggered another burst of pain which made him shiver.

The man did not move. Their faces were now only a few centimetres apart but Orestis could still not really see him.

'A religious cutter!' he exclaimed. 'Interesting. Aren't you afraid you're going to burn in hell or something?'

'It's just a figure of speech, you creep,' Orestis replied. The initial surprise now gave way to anger. He banged his fist on the wall. 'How about you fuck off and give me some privacy?'

The man still made no attempt to budge. 'I just don't get it,' he went on.

Orestis realised he wasn't going to leave him alone. 'What's that?' he sighed, hoping he could get rid of him more quickly if he played along for a little while.

'Well, this, for starters.' He pointed to his left, in the direction of the meeting room. 'The need to talk away your pain. The "this is a safe space" bullshit.' He imitated Marios's slow way of speaking. 'It's nothing but an echo chamber. What's the point of healing' – he put his palms together and bowed his head like a Tibetan monk – 'in a vacuum only to go back to real life and find yourself buried in shit again? If you are in pain, you don't "talk", you take back control, you stop pitying yourself and do something about it!'

'Then why are *you* here?' Orestis asked.

'Judge's orders,' the man just said. 'You?'

'None of your damn business.'

The man snorted. His shoes squeaked on the porcelain toilet seat in the next cubicle as he leaned closer. 'And this?' he said, extending his arm and tapping Orestis' forehead, making him take a step back. 'Cutting numbs your mind only temporarily. You want to get rid of the voices? You've got to try something else.'

'Like what?' Orestis said casually, but he was intrigued.

The man jumped down and went to stand outside Orestis' cubicle. Orestis could see his shadow below the door, waiting. He picked up the bloodied razor blade from the floor before undoing the latch and coming face to face with the dark figure hiding behind the hood. He was a few centimetres taller than Orestis – probably around two metres – and had a muscular build.

'You listen to them. Accept they are a part of you now. Always will be,' he said.

'You're crazy,' Orestis replied dismissively, but something in the man's words resonated with him. A short pause. 'Did *you*?' he finally asked. 'Quiet the voices?'

The man removed his hood. He revealed a disfigured face full of scars which created craters and pits on his veiny skin from his neck to his ear to the back of his skull where hair now grew only in patches. His right eye was almost covered by swollen flesh and only a small part of its iris was visible.

Orestis' wide open eyes lingered on the grotesque sight a little more that they should have. Meeting the man's gaze, he could tell he was used to this reaction. He turned his eyes to the floor, embarrassed, then, unable to resist, to the man's reflection in the mirror. It was easier that way.

'I'm working on it,' the man said with a sad look on his face.

'How did you...?' Orestis started, but couldn't finish his question.

The man cupped his hand around the nape of Orestis' neck.

'Some of us don't get pissed on, mate. Just pissed off.'

CHAPTER 1
National Independence Day
Sunday 25 March 2018

The penetrating sound of the alarm clock brought Ares out of his dream of yesterday's late-night meeting in the office and back to his bedroom. Ten to nine. Shit, he was going to be late for the parade. He hadn't seen Orestis for a year. He knew how important this day was for his brother, he didn't want to screw it up.

He jumped out of bed, picked up his shirt and jeans from the floor and fumbled under the sheets for his phone. That was when he noticed the yellow Post-it note on the left side of the bed.

'Had to go. Don't call.'

I wasn't going to, Ares thought, looking at the cursive handwriting. He crumpled the paper into a tiny ball and threw it in the bin. Why did he always have to be the one feeling guilty the day after? He suppressed the thought, he had to hurry.

When he finally found his phone, he saw that he'd had four missed calls from Orestis, three from around midnight last night and one from four-thirty this morning. There was a voicemail from him too. At first, Ares thought it was blank as he could only hear the hissing sound of the wind. He was about to hang up when he heard his brother saying his name, then a curt 'See you tomorrow' before ending the message.

A new wave of guilt hit him. Why hadn't he checked his phone sooner? Why was he wasting his time with people who didn't deserve it and neglecting those who mattered to him the most? Orestis was probably only looking for some words of encouragement from him before his first parade as a presidential guard and Ares had let him down. Again. He tried calling him back but there was no reply.

He got dressed as quickly as he could and took a taxi to downtown Athens. He managed to arrive at Syntagma Square just before ten o'clock.

People of all ages had gathered on the left and right side of Amalias Avenue, most of them dressed in blue and white and waving Greek flags in anticipation. The normally busy Athenian street was now devoid of traffic except for the police and emergency vehicles parked on the side roads. Police officers were the only ones crossing the street to make sure everything was in order for the parade to start.

Ares was wondering whether he had time to go grab a coffee from the nearest Starbucks when he felt his phone vibrating in his pocket.

Irene.

Before he had the chance to open his mouth, his editor's cigarette-roughened voice filled his ears.

'Ares, at last! I need the sex trafficking piece cut down to a thousand before it goes to print and an even shorter version – around seven hundred – for the website.'

'Good morning to you too, Irene,' he said sarcastically. They'd been working together at Argo Press for seven years now. Irene was hardly the bossy type, and they'd soon become friends. But even after all this time, Ares hadn't got fully used to how differently he and Irene saw things like work or life in general. He was a marathon runner, Irene was a sprinter. 'I finished them yesterday after the meeting. They're both in your inbox.'

'You're a star, I'll check them later. Where did you disappear to last night? I came by your office around quarter past two but you were gone.'

'I was sleeping like a baby by that time,' he lied. 'I was knackered.'

From where he was standing, Ares saw the Ministers of Defence and Education arriving. The President and the Archbishop of Athens were also on the VIP stand in front of the Parliament. The speakers that had been set up on the lamp posts across the street made a static buzz as they were switched on. *And so the show begins.* Distracted by the whirl of activity around him, Ares forgot he was still on the phone.

'Where the hell are you?' Irene said. 'What's that noise?'

'It's called the national anthem, my dear, and that's a sign that you probably haven't been to a parade since your school days,' Ares said jokingly, covering his left ear with his palm to shut out the noise.

'Fuck, I forgot. It's the Andreou brothers' big reunion today, isn't it?'

'I told you, it's a little thing we used to do with our mother,' Ares said.

'Ah, yes, the good old days. Feeling nostalgic, are we, Mr Andreou?'

Turning his gaze to the procession, Ares saw the first group of paraders approaching, students from all the Athenian high schools. His eyes met those of the short, chubby girl in the front row struggling under the weight of the flag she was carrying. Her head soon turned to Ares' right, where a man of a similar round build was waving at her with a camera in his hand.

'Feeling old, more likely,' Ares replied. 'Orestis was obsessed with presidential guards as a kid and now here he is, a presidential guard himself.' He smiled, not so much because of what a great honour it was to be in the guard – he didn't really care about these things – but because he knew how much this meant to Orestis. *My little brother, a presidential guard, an Evzonas.* Tourists would observe him while on guard, queue up to take photos with him, tease him to see if he could keep his expressionless face. Their mother would have burst with pride.

Irene said something, but her words were lost in the whooshing sound of the two F16 fighter jets doing their manoeuvring show in the sky. Ares asked her to speak up.

'Can you hear me now?' she asked. 'Does this mean you're back on speaking terms with Orestis?'

Ares sighed. 'Sort of. It's hard after all these years, you know? He's still keeping me at arm's length, but it's a start.'

Even over the phone, Irene probably felt he wasn't as confident about it as he was trying to sound because she said, 'How many times do I have to say this, Ares? It wasn't your fault. You were just a kid, you both were. He'll realise that one day.'

Ares nodded even though Irene wasn't there to see him. When she wasn't caught up in her own little web of ample smoking and swearing, last-minute deadlines and all-too-young boyfriends from hell, his friend knew exactly what to say to make him feel better.

The last parading students were disappearing down Panepistimiou Avenue. Ares heard the heavy, rhythmic march of the *evzones*. 'Irene, got to go. The evzones are coming. See you in the office later?'

'No need to come in, just go be with your brother. Oh, one last thing. Rania should be there somewhere doing a piece for the website. Have you seen her?'

'No, she's probably at the media stand. I'm on the other side of Amalias.'

'No worries, I'll tell her to get a close-up of the other Andreou brother. No way he can be uglier than you, so we might use it for the story.'

'Love you too, Irene,' Ares chuckled. 'Leave my brother alone.'

'Speak soon, gorgeous,' Irene said, also laughing, and hung up.

The evzones were getting closer now, following the marching orders the chief commander to their right was giving at the top of his voice.

The sight brought Ares back to his teenage years and one of his early morning discussions with Orestis about the guards' strange-looking uniforms. 'Did you know,' he'd said in his shrill child's voice, 'that the tsarouchia the evzones wear weigh one kilo each and have sixty nails on their soles? Or that their skirt of four hundred pleats, the foustanella, represents the four hundred years of Ottoman occupation? Mrs Spanou told us in history class!'

Ares still remembered the spark of fascination in his little brother's bleary eyes. Damn, how he missed the long-lost simplicity of those days.

Where is he? Ares wondered, getting more and more anxious with every minute that passed. *Have I missed him in the crowd?* He was taller than many of those around him, but still couldn't spot Orestis among the sea of raised phones and waving flags. He'd kept away from the elevated media stand before the Tomb of the Unknown Soldier – where he knew Rania and other fellow journalists would be – to avoid meaningless small talk, but he now wasn't sure this had been wise.

He tried to move closer to the street to get to a better viewpoint, but the crowd was too absorbed in the spectacle to let him through. While making his way to the front, he sensed some of the onlookers staring in the usual *Is he? Isn't he?* way and whispering to the person next to them.

A twenty-something woman with a beehive hairstyle grabbed his arm and, shoving her phone in his face, asked, 'A selfie?'

'Sorry, not today,' he replied a little more gruffly than he'd intended.

He freed his arm from her grip and kept moving.

'What a snob!' he heard her say to her friend in a loud voice as he was walking away.

He finally managed to reach the front row, as close to the wreath-laying site in front of the Parliament as civilians could get. And then he saw Orestis in the second group of evzones now approaching the VIP stand. It took a while to recognise his brother. *What did you expect? You haven't seen him for a year.* He'd shaved his beard and his once round cheeks were now hollowed. His red fez was covering most of his dark, curly hair.

Observing Orestis' controlled body movements reminded Ares of a game they used to play during their last summer together. One of them would pretend to be a Schwarzenegger-like robot while the other was telling jokes and making funny faces, trying to make the robot laugh. Orestis would always laugh first and nothing pleased Ares more than seeing his little brother happy.

Distracted by those thoughts, Ares needed a few seconds to locate the source of the growing disquiet around him.

An evzonas from the fourth row of the second group.

Orestis?

An evzonas that suddenly broke the marching line.

Orestis.

An apostate.

Orestis!

Ares felt his heart racing in his chest. Everything happened so fast and yet in his mind it registered as if in slow motion.

In the moments that followed, when everyone was trying to figure out what was going on and whether this was part of the parade routine, Orestis turned right at the same marching pace. He left Amalias Avenue and entered the pedestrian zone in front of the Parliament where the VIP and media stands were.

The surprised faces and reactions of the other evzones suggested that whatever was happening had not been rehearsed. Some guards kept marching to the opposite side, following their initial orders although the chief commander had stopped giving any. Others, unable to decide what to do, turned back and started heading in Orestis' direction. Orestis was now getting closer to President Panagiotidis and the Ministers.

'Andreou, stop!' an authoritative voice shouted from somewhere behind

Ares but if Orestis had heard the order, he showed no intention to follow it. Cameras were flashing everywhere, Ares' colleagues at the media stand were loving it.

What the hell is he doing? Ares wondered. This wasn't like Orestis. His brother needed him. He'd no doubt have a lot of explaining to do for this, maybe even go through a court martial. Ares had to stand by him, help him get his side across – whatever that was.

He was being jostled by the bodies of evzones, soldiers, police officers, journalists and spectators running to or away from the scene like ants whose colony had just been trampled on. As he approached the centre of the commotion, he saw Orestis stopping in front of the Tomb of the Unknown Soldier, a few steps away from the VIP stand. He was standing still, looking at Panagiotidis's wrinkled, shocked face.

Orestis took the rifle he'd been carrying on his left shoulder and placed it at his feet. The move put the President's security guards on alert. They covered Panagiotidis with their bodies and drew their guns.

Orestis removed his hat, wiped his eyes with the back of his palm and then quickly lifted the rifle, putting the muzzle in his mouth.

Ares froze at the realisation of what his brother was about to do. He had to act fast, to stop him before it was too late, but his body had gone numb. 'Orestis, don't!' he managed to yell at the top of his lungs from where he was, but his words were lost in a sea of panicked voices, radio orders, sirens and screeching tyres.

A gunshot echoed across Syntagma Square.

People say your whole life flashes before your eyes when you die, but the same goes for those you've shared precious moments with as they watch you take your last breath.

Running at full speed, Ares saw the little boy who once called him *Alles,* unable to pronounce his name and who refused to go to bed unless he tucked him in, fall backwards, rifle still in hands.

In the blink of an eye, the nostalgic recollection of those days was wiped away by regret for the new memories that never would be – and the guilt that came with it. For the promise Ares had given to his brother always to be there for him, never to let anyone else hurt him, was now forever broken. It was this guilt, soon turned into self-disgust and then sheer anger, that forced his body out of its momentary paralysis.

With the first tears running down his face, Ares tried to break through the line of police officers blocking his way. He didn't see the truncheon coming. A sharp pain seized his ribcage, taking his breath away. Then a sudden push with a shield knocked him over. He landed on his back. Invisible hands rolled him over and held him to the ground.

He begged the officers to save his brother, to call an ambulance, to do something, he threatened them, cursed them, kicked them.

Then he realised the futility of it all and stopped, resigned. Still on his chest, Ares stretched his neck to get a better look at the immobile body between the disembodied legs running around. His brother was lying on his side a few metres away. Blood had started soaking his white uniform and a pool had formed around his head like a scarlet halo. Red drops were rolling down the white marble of the Tomb of the Unknown Soldier, following the direction of the inscribed letters:

The whole earth is the burial ground of famous men.

Orestis' eyes were still open. Ares would swear they were looking at him. They would always be looking at him.

Denise Beardon is a security awareness consultant interested in exploring the interaction between human behaviour and technology. Working on international cyber security awareness programmes, she educates people on how to protect themselves from cyber crime. Denise lives in Cambridgeshire with her family. *Do Not Assume* is her first crime novel.

spiritweave@hotmail.co.uk

Do Not Assume

The young Asian girl twirled on the computer screen. Her dark blue silk scarf gathered pace with each spin; the diamonds sparkled then blurred, lighting her up with a full-body halo. I watched mesmerised. A Bollywood tune blared from her computer's speakers, the same song playing on repeat. She danced with abandon. A release. A private moment, which no one should have seen. Except here I was on the other side of the monitor. Watching.

Shafia was a computer science undergraduate. Born in Wolverhampton, she was the eldest of three and the first of her siblings to go to university. And she hadn't gone in half-hearted, she had hit the big time. Cambridge. Which meant she was smart, stellar-smart.

I watched as she sweated her stuff in the confines of her room. Her right arm bent towards her hip; her left arm held above her head – each hand was curled into a mudra position. She mouthed the lyrics of the song, her face drawn into an *O* expression.

Shafia paused and extended her leg, motionless in mid-flight. She adopted a defensive position and turned kick-box warrior, her chin slanted down, her eyes looking towards the bedroom door. Every muscle was held taut, ready for release; the swing of her high ponytail the only movement. I heard someone knocking on the door.

Her face turned towards the monitor screen, and she looked through me, above and below. A cup of tea was slid into place on my desk. I nodded my thanks, but kept my eyes fixed on my suspect. Her foot slammed to the floor, and she reached towards the monitor, turning the music off.

'All right, all right!' Shafia opened the door, unwinding the silk fabric from around her shoulders. She greeted the young woman, 'Hey, Rom,' and stood to one side to let her in.

Romola entered the room and threw the straw boater hat she'd been wearing onto the bed, releasing a mass of short blonde curls. A regular visitor, the two women were close friends.

'Bloody tourists.' Romola started unbuttoning her waistcoat and slipped off her shoes.

'Now what?' Shafia asked.

'There I am, giving it everything about the Mathematical Bridge when some woman from another punt tries to get into mine.' Romola tapped her head. 'Said her boat was sinking. Fucking chaos.'

'What did you do?'

'The only thing I could do. I defended my customers with my oar.' Shafia looked shocked, but Romola nudged her and laughed. 'I'm surprised none of us ended up in the drink.'

They both laughed then sat down on the bed, pushing themselves back to lean on the wall. The door left open, another student wandered in.

As my lower back started to lock, I felt the urge to stand, but the lead on the headphones they had given me was too short. Doubtless part of the rookie's initiation and something I could have done without. I thumbed over Shafia's photo in the hard copy file. The image, lifted from her Instagram account, was pixelated.

Baby-faced at nineteen years old, her wide chocolate brown eyes looked up innocently from beneath the rim of a white fur hat. No matter how harmless she looked, Shafia was a listed terrorist suspect. Following a fatal school fire, believed to have been started by a printer, the tiny microchip found in the charred remains of the building pointed to her. Taking place out of hours, the students were safe, but, Lena, a twenty-two-year-old cleaner listening to her headphones while she worked, had perished. Oblivious to the fire alarm and overcome by thick toxic smoke, she had passed out before dying, her melted plastic headphones left welded to her blackened corpse.

When the recovered microchip was analysed, Shafia's computer IP address had lit up like a digital beacon. Meaning she or someone using her computer's identity had pulled the remote trigger deliberately, overheating the school printer, which caused the fire. The brief for the investigation described Shafia as British-Muslim. There was a high chance she had been radicalised, and my commander feared she would act again.

So, there I was, with permission to enter and observe the young student, using the most intimate surveillance, for as long as it took to bring her to justice. And even though she was my first, something didn't feel right.

CHAPTER TWO

For years, counter terrorism units around the world had seen an increase in the number of fatal terrorist bombs organised and planted by women. Recruited by fundamentalists, indiscriminate of age, sometimes the girls were as young as fifteen. I stopped staring at Shafia's dark oval eyes and glossy-lipped smile and pulled my attention back to the report.

This was the tenth fire to have been caused by a Textonics printer in Europe and North America in the past six months. Initially, the company had suspected a fault in production and started to recall batch models to stem a potentially huge PR disaster. But when they discovered that their printers were only catching fire in schools, any suspicion of a fault in the manufacturing components was ruled out. Finding a link to Shafia was Operation Piper's first real breakthrough.

I'd only been investigating Shafia for a few weeks, but she seemed more interested in clothes and fake eyelashes than the five prayers. Her Instagram and Facebook accounts were full of pouting and posturing selfies. One of Shafia in a dress, the next in a jumpsuit; her hips tilted to the left and her looking back over her shoulder. Hair worn curly, hair worn straight, then an up-do. There were only a few images of her wearing a hijab, and I'd found nothing to link her to fundamentalism.

'Where are you hiding it?' I muttered under my breath.

Khalil's head appeared from behind the office divider. He remained seated on his chair and scooted across to me: the wheels scraping against the wooden flooring.

'Still not getting anywhere with your black widow spider?' Khalil said.

I put her Facebook images on the screen. 'I'm not sure she'd eat you for breakfast, but she does have the appearance of being a little too perfect.'

'She's the most glamorous geek I've seen,' he smiled, leaning his elbows on my desk.

'True... until you see her Bollywood moves. She should stick to coding.'

'Well, Josh is convinced Shafia's the key to all this, so I guess you are going to have to prove it.'

'Any luck with yours?'

'You think you've got problems. I've never seen such a mess.' He caught me looking at his dishevelled shirt and laughed. There were loose tufts sticking out of his tightly curled hair and I could smell a hint of garlic on his breath. Khalil had pulled an all-nighter. 'What have you got on her, so far?'

'Not much. Here, let me show you.' I moved the mouse across the screen and scanned the Cambridge University website looking for Shafia's computer science degree. I left the cursor resting on a subgroup: quantum computing.

'The holy grail of cyber security,' Khalil said.

'Exactly. This level of computing could take years for Shafia to get to. But if she wanted to, she could charm the lecturers to give her early access to all the material. Once she figures out quantum, she'll be streets ahead of us in terms of hacking.'

Khalil pointed to her image. 'I called her the black widow spider for a good reason. I reckon she could be lethal if she wanted to be.'

'There's something else. As part of the degree, in her second year our very own National Cyber Security Centre will offer her a short secondment to work with them.'

'But that means she must have got the right security clearance to start with.'

'Which we both know means nothing. After all, you passed it.' I stood up, just as his hand swotted the air in my direction. I looked beyond the window at the large flat arable fields stretching into the distance. Part of the newly formed counter terrorism cyber intelligence unit, our anonymous monochrome office, located on the corner of the Cambridge Science Park, at least afforded us with a view. Unlike the giant RAF bunker that housed most of the Ministry of Defence's intel services less than 20 miles away.

The sun setting, Khalil's self-imposed 24-hour shift was coming to an end. He stood up next to me. 'Forget Shafia's Facebook messages and Instagram. Look at the skill she uses when she codes. That might be where you find the real Shafia, not this social media goddess.'

Shafia spent the next couple of hours applying heavy black liner to her eyes, curling her hair and painting her nails. It made me think of my fifteen-year-old daughter, Melissa, painting her toenails while sat among the floordrobe she seemed to accumulate each week in her bedroom. I wouldn't see her that night, having asked to take the night shift.

American Bob, my 24-hour job share, always left me his notes and observations, and sometimes recorded footage from the previous evening, but nothing beat witnessing a target in real time. Only suspected terrorists deserved this level of observation and the interception warrant had been signed off by the highest level of authority: the Home Office. I looked at the girl on the screen tarting herself up and wondered if she knew how much trouble she was in.

Shafia left the room at 9pm, leaving the overhead light switched on. The space was suddenly empty and flat, the silence eerie. I switched on the remote access to zoom in through the webcam for a closer inspection. Less disruptive than a physical search; if I found enough evidence to warrant it that would be our next step.

The lens provided me with a good view of her halls of residence bedroom; only the furthest left-hand corner and the desk that the webcam sat on were lost to me. Her unmade single bed was opposite. I could see part of a wardrobe, its doors ajar, reflected in a mirror. The wardrobe was filled with deep greens, blues and dark magentas. I heard someone cough behind me in the office but ignored them. I didn't know how long I had before Shafia returned.

Above her bed was a dark blue noticeboard. Regardless of the arrival of digital media, the photo montage was alive and well, with the left-hand side of the board a sea of faces. Using the same system as the fingertip searches I'd learnt as a PC, I made sure that the noticeboard received the same level of scrutiny. There were plenty of group shots; any one of them could be a person of interest.

I scanned through the pinned images, taking in each line, recognising her mum, dad, sister, brother. Her parents were married and settled in the UK. Both qualified chemists, their local pharmacy business appeared to be doing well. Growing up, she'd had several aunts, uncles and cousins living close by. The family showed no signs of trouble, apart from at a far-right protest the previous year. Her cousin had headbutted a police officer, breaking his nose, which rewarded him with a caution and a night in the cells. There was also a picture of Shafia and Romola on the noticeboard, and some of her other friends from her Facebook account.

Shafia had stuck random scattered papers on the right of the notice board. I scanned them for any fundamentalist propaganda or clippings from the magazine *Rumiyah*. Sticking out from beneath the overlapped layers, the corner of a leaflet caught my attention. The font was small but familiar. I zoomed in further. Did that say 'tonics'?

A hand shot into view from the bedroom door snapping the light switch off. The room was plunged into darkness. The door lock turned signalling that my live search was over.

Her Twitter and Facebook accounts gave me no hints as to where she had gone. The next step was to target her mobile phone. While I had time, I set about creating a convincing email using our phishing simulation software. One of its special edition Christmas templates, the new John Lewis advert caught my eye. Shafia may have been Muslim, but I didn't know anyone who wouldn't fall for that cheese. If she tapped on its link, it would trigger a Trojan virus on her device, giving me access to her mobile. I sat back and admired my handiwork. There were other ways, but this was tried and tested. As long as she clicked on that link.

With the room empty and dark, there was nothing else to do but wait, so I went to the kitchen and microwaved my meal for one. I was spooling a strand of rubbery pasta around my fork when Josh appeared.

'What's happening with Shafia?'

'Just my luck, she's gone out. I'm not sure where or what time she'll return either. I think I've found something of interest on her noticeboard though. It could be a link to the printer, but I'm not sure. I could do with a second opinion.'

'OK, notify me when she's back.' He tapped the countertop hard twice, then walked out.

I stared at where Josh's knuckles had struck the wood. l hadn't got the measure of our commander yet, but there was no doubt I found the man irritating. Maybe the feeling was mutual. To date, my policing had taken place in the shires, while Josh had made his way up through the ranks of the Metropolitan Police working in special ops for Organised Crime and now Counter Terrorism. He probably didn't think I was good enough for this new venture.

As I forced the watery carbonara into my mouth, my mind drifted to the dark place and my preoccupation with the possibility of failure. It wasn't just the prospect of letting an extremist escape that was getting to me. As a single mum, I needed the money. Now that Ray was eighteen, the maintenance payments from my ex were half of what I was used to, even though I was still sending our son handouts to help keep him afloat at university.

I chided myself – I wasn't the only one feeling the pressure. Our covert operation, the brainchild of the UK's newly appointed chief of counter terrorism had only been underway for a matter of months. The chief had chosen Cambridge to provide the unit with the quickest access to the most intelligent minds in the country. Home to Silicon Fen and some of the most innovative tech companies in the world, surrounded by top military intelligence units and with the support of an award-winning university department, the location was textbook for what we needed. The truth was that until we proved our worth, every one of us was still on probation. And while we had the keen eyes of the Chief and the Home Office upon us, there was simply no room for error.

Shafia arrived back in her room in the early hours of the morning. She swayed as she removed her coat and scarf, putting them on the coat hook. Her usual immaculate appearance was in disarray, her lipstick smudged.

'What the hell happened to you?' I said.

Her entrance into the bedroom was followed by a sharp knock on the door and the sound of a male voice coming from the corridor outside.

I started to drum my fingers on the desk.

Shafia stood by the door. She was wearing a tight pencil skirt and a black top with silver diamonds. Kicking her heels off, she turned the key in the door to lock it and pushed the bolt across. The man's voice spoke again, but his words were indecipherable. He thumped on the door.

She ignored him and dropped her keys to the floor, walking towards the bed. Five minutes later Shafia Khan was asleep on her bed fully clothed. She had left the lights on.

I rubbed my hands together. 'You beauty,' I said, focusing the camera lens back onto the noticeboard. I buzzed Josh to join me; I was impatient to show him my 'tonics' find.

'She took her sweet-ass time,' Josh was bleary-eyed.

I nodded towards his corner office. 'Sofa not that comfy then?'

'Ha, bloody ha.'

'Hold on. Shh.'

I raised my finger to my lips, gesturing him to pick up the spare headset. He grumbled. With no time to grab a chair, and only a short cable on the spare headset, he was forced to kneel on the floor.

It sounded like someone was in Shafia's room. Undisturbed, she lay dormant on the bed, the diamonds on her blouse twinkling as she breathed. I searched the shadows for movement but couldn't see anyone.

'Let yourself go,' a disembodied male voice said. 'As you exhale, silently say to yourself the word *calm* or any other word you might find relaxing.'

'Did she switch on a meditation app or something?' Josh asked.

I shrugged.

There was the sound of birds tweeting, and panpipes playing in the distance; it reminded me of a beauty spa.

The voice continued. 'As you take a deep breath in, Shafia, let the feelings of relaxation wash over you, as if you are in a warm bath.'

'What the fuck?' I mouthed at Josh before raising my pen and pointing out the line of code on my monitor screen. 'This is not an application,' I said. 'Shafia's got an intruder.'

The voice was suddenly taken over by a high-pitched whistle accompanied by white noise as if a radio was out of tune. The noise was piercing, and we both wrenched the headphones away from our ears. Shafia stirred, lifted herself from the bed and pulled at the cables under the desk. The noise persisted. She returned to the bed wrapping the pillow around her ears.

'Why doesn't she switch it off?' asked Josh.

'I don't think she can.'

CHAPTER THREE

The front door banged as it was slammed open, waking me with a jolt. Melissa was back from school. I rearranged my legs around the cushions cocooning me in the large suede sofa. The all-nighter had taken its toll; I hadn't made it upstairs.

'Mum?' Melissa hollered, almost ripping the downstairs cloakroom door off its hinges.

'Hey Missy,' I called before listening to my daughter pee. 'Do you hold it in all day?'

October had brought a warm glow to the garden and I let my gaze soften on the burnt orange leaves carpeting the lawn beyond the patio doors. I pulled the woollen grey throw under my chin. Arriving back at 8:00am, I'd managed a full day's sleep.

The toilet flushed.

A long curl of brown hair wafted over my face, as Melissa planted a wet kiss on my forehead, and ruffled my hair. I squirmed.

'There was no hand wash at school again today.' Melissa's daily complaint was the poor state of health of the girls' loos.

'I hope you washed your hands then?'

'Here, smell?' A wet hand hovered near my chin. An old routine from her earlier childhood, which had worked at the time, was now just unpleasant. I reminded myself not to ask next time.

'Yes, all right. That's not necessary.'

Melissa walked around to the front of the sofa and sat down on the carpet. She tilted her head to one side.

'You haven't forgotten, have you?'

'How do you get your eyes to look that big?'

'Mum, don't, you haven't forgotten, right? I know you've had a long week, I know you're tired, but I am still going, aren't I? It's just Katie will be mad at me if I pull out for another year.'

I let her prattle on, my mind allowing the small glow-worm of a memory to work its way back into focus. Melissa held her arm across her face, mimicking wearing a cloak.

'Bollocks, it's bloody Halloween, isn't it? Oh bugger, what time is it? You're going out... a party? A sleepover or something.'

'Yes, at Katie's, remember?'

'Don't you girls want to stay here tonight? You were away last night.'

'Nah, Katie won't want to.'

'Why's that?'

'Because of Vincent.' Missy was casual in the way she said the name, but a tiny movement in the corner of her mouth, told me something else. It was the first time I'd heard his name.

'So, tell me about this Vincent.'

She lifted herself from the floor and sat on the other sofa, waiting until I had sat up and twisted round to face her.

'He's this gamer that Katie's made friends with online. I didn't mind at first, but now she's on Skype to him all the time and she's even stopped playing *League of Legends*.'

'How old is he?'

'Same age, I think.'

I doubted Katie's online friend was fifteen.

'How long has she known him?'

'They've known each other a couple of years.'

'That means she would have been about thirteen when they first started talking. And Katie doesn't know him. Have you met him?'

Missy glanced at me. 'No, Katie won't let me.'

'If she is on Skype all the time to him, what do you do when you're staying over?'

'Go to the box room. Play games on my mobile.'

I felt a sharp twist of guilt and struggled to look at her. If it wasn't for the night shifts I'd insisted on taking, Missy wouldn't have to put up with it. Life was so much easier before Ray went to uni.

'I'm sorry to hear that. It sounds like Katie is being a bit mean. Are you sure you still want to go tonight?'

'Yeah, it's a sleepover. It won't be just me tonight,' she glanced at her watch. 'I've got to get ready, it's fancy dress. You said you'd help straighten my hair.'

Forty minutes later and after I'd managed to singe one of my fingers on the straighteners, Missy set off for Katie's house on the other side of the village. An overnight bag slung across her shoulder, she pinned her black cape to her front. I noted the black fishnet tights and red high heels poking from underneath the black cloth but didn't say anything. After all, she was going to Katie's, there wasn't much she could get up to there.

For the next hour, I was visited by various mini-incarnations of Harry Potter characters, hastily bandaged mummies and one pre-pubescent Poison Ivy. I dished out the sweets with a smile, secretly cursing the parents for knocking on my door.

When the stash of sweets ran out, I retreated into the lounge, turning off the lights at the front of the house to make it look empty. I poured a large glass of brandy and switched on the laptop. I called Ray on Skype and laughed as my son's face emerged, covered in white face paint.

'Don't tell me. Dracula?'

He grinned. 'Muah ha ha. How did you guess?'

'Because your sister has just gone out wearing a cloak. I swear to God you two have got a thing about capes.'

'Oh yeah, the fancy dress party. That's at Katie's house, isn't it?'

'Yeah, how did you know? Have you been speaking to Missy?' I was surprised; the two of them had always kept their distance growing up.

'It does happen, Mum.' He started touching his hair, checking himself out in the Skype's self-view window. 'Anyway, I've got my own party tonight.'

I managed to keep Ray talking for another ten minutes before losing him to his mates as they piled into his room. Halloween was always the same. Both my children revelled in the celebration while I preferred to avoid it. I flicked on the TV, ate some dinner and drank more brandy.

I must have fallen asleep as some hours later I woke to find myself lying on the sofa with my mobile buzzing next to me. Even though I was groggy, and my head was thick with drink, I swiped on the green receive button.

'Alex, you got five?' I recognised the southern accent of my black American counterpart, Bob. Thinking about how good he looked, part of me wished this was a social call, until I remembered he was married. I dragged myself up and headed for the kitchen. I needed water.

'Yeah, sure.'

'It's about this hacker business with Shafia. Josh is giving me a load of heat saying I must have missed it, but I swear to you the hacking must have just started. I wouldn't miss something like that.'

'I'm guessing you haven't come across it before?' I reached the kitchen, put Bob on loudspeaker, and filled a tumbler with water, before glugging it down.

'That's the problem. I've been watching the girl just the same as you, but I haven't heard nothing. Josh has given me a load of crap tonight. Even accused me of falling asleep.' Bob paused. 'How the hell did you find this hacker?'

Bob was originally from Biloxi, Tennessee and was normally a laid-back southern honey type. No fool, but not one to get strung up over nothing. At six foot three, I didn't know many people who would risk pissing him off. I had never heard him so agitated. I sensed his frustration but at the back of my mind, I wondered if Josh was right.

'When we heard the man's voice last night, at first Josh thought it might be some sort of meditation or sleep app. I started to look for the source code and that's when I saw that Shafia's desktop had been opened by a remote access virus. That's how I think the intruder got in and how they were controlling her audio and video. The hack was tricky to see though. I could see the code in the task bar, but even then, I was only guessing.'

'Hmm, maybe that's why Josh has gone and got himself an opinion. I couldn't believe what I was hearing. It's not how we do things back home, but maybe that's the point of all this swapping people around.'

'Who's on shift with her now?'

'No one, Alex.'

'Excuse me?'

'That's why I'm calling. Josh has ditched all surveillance on Shafia.'

'But, why? She's guilty.'

'You and I know that, but Josh is under pressure from the Home Office. It's been weeks and there is not enough evidence to carry on with the investigation. We haven't found any other connection to Shafia and that damned school fire, apart from some unfortunate IP link. We could spend an age watching this kid. And Josh, well let's just say he no longer has the backing.'

'Wow, that's it then?' I'm incredulous. 'What about the intruder?'

Bob sighed. 'Josh said, and I quote, "if Alex wants to save this girl from some nasty little stalker, she needs to go back to neighbourhood policing. We're looking for the organised, the big guns, not some creep who gets his rocks off telling bedtime stories to sleeping beauty." It's all about the terrorism.'

Smarting at his words, I walked back to the sofa and poured another brandy. It bothered me that Josh had missed the point. The hacker was a key lead in the investigation and may have had something to do with the printer fires. On the night of his discovery, I'd wanted to do a hack back, which would have meant following the hacker's digital trail to find him, but Josh had stopped me.

'A dead end then. Thanks for letting me know.' I closed the call, too irritated to trust myself to discuss it any further. The hacker incident had felt significant, and I was sure Josh had felt the same when I left him. I didn't understand why the guilty party was about to be let off. Nobody was watching Shafia, but that didn't mean I couldn't.

If I could just watch her for a bit longer; check her emails and texts, I might find that connection and possibly prevent another fire.

Now she was no longer a person of interest I'd be stepping outside of my remit. And without the interception warrant's protection, I'd be operating on the wrong side of the law.

I swilled the last dregs of brandy around the bottom of the glass. Officially, I didn't know her surveillance had been stopped and I wasn't due to find out until Monday morning. That gave me another twenty-four hours to play with. I woke the laptop from sleep mode.

The screen blinked into action and I remote logged into the office server to see if any connection had been made with Shafia. She had ignored my previous phishing email. If I was going to catch her, I was going to have to be a lot smarter. I opened up her Facebook page.

Bob Jones was born and brought up in Monmouthshire, but now divides his time between Snowdonia and Buckinghamshire. He has enjoyed a 30-year career in local, national and international broadcasting in the UK, Belgium, and China. He hosts shows on Classic FM, and is a journalist for BFBS/Forces News.

bob@bobjonesmedia.com

Quarry

A quarry full of bones. You have to wonder how it all started. Or was it ever thus. Bones picked clean of flesh by ravenous animals and birds.

Long before the caverns and waste heaps came to define the valley, a natural fracture in the land provided a useful place for the disposal of the inconvenient.

The smallest bones belong to babies. The unwanted. Spared the pain of making sense of a world they had so briefly been born into. Taken from disconsolate mothers by 'wise women' in the village, who would insist that, if they had been allowed to live, then they would have brought nothing but pain and poverty to their already impoverished families. At the jaws of the pit the child would be held aloft as a prayer was mumbled, before being dropped. They would listen, waiting for one last cry. But why should it? A baby never knows it's about to die. Everything in its life is new. Death an unknown concept. As the infant fell, perhaps it would hear with fascination the echo of tumbling rocks, and maybe the sound of water disturbed somewhere down below, water that eventually and suddenly would envelop them and bring darkness.

To keep the curious away, children were told the pit was the Palace of the Devil, and that He was waiting for those just like them – curious, adventuresome – who dared to follow the path to the edge of the quarry and stare down into the soul of the earth. Occasionally, some lost their footing, and stepped into eternity; the pit was deemed too dangerous to attempt a rescue, even if you could hear desperate calls coming from below. More likely, the task would have been to retrieve a lifeless body. What was the point of descending into hell to bring back a body which would then be placed in the earth once again? So, they left them where they were. Sometimes prayers were said as close as people dared get.

In a remarkably short time, the child would be forgotten. Only occasionally brought to mind when a mother, now a grandmother, was tallying regrets, like counting stitches, in her later years, waiting for her own death, and the chance to meet her child again.

Centuries of miners added their bones to the calciferous hoard. Left where they fell. 'Let them rest with the devil,' the owners would say. 'Death there was surely better than their lives above ground.'

And after the quarry closed, a spring at its base took possession. Inch by inch, it filled with water from the spring till it found its own level, some fifty feet below the pit edge. Yellow gorse and saplings insisted on smothering the symmetry of the slate. The quarry was destined to keep its secrets and stored souls for evermore.

Apart from one. A recent convert to eternity. Bound and gagged, wrapped in a tarpaulin and weighted with a breeze block, it had been hurled into the dead centre of the pit. Self-congratulatory hands were slapped together as a sign of a job well done, backs turned to the deed as they headed down to the pub, never to speak of this act again, unless it was with their eyes alone.

And so, almost twenty years to the day, one lonely forgotten body let slip its bonds, and drifted slowly but irrevocably to the surface. All the souls of the innocent babies, the careless children and the luckless miners turned their passionless eyes to watch it rise. They felt no jealousy. Maybe a sense of curiosity. What would the living make of the escapee from oblivion? What mischief would it cause?

CHAPTER TWO

It took a full sixty seconds for the sound of heavy yet careful departing footsteps on the steep stairway to fade. And then a further minute of intent listening before the inhabitant of the room felt confident enough to go about its business undisturbed. A cramped attic flat, at the very top of a jaded Georgian building, in a neglected side street just off the seafront, behind one of Llandudno's grand hotels, but not *The* Grand. So many layers of paint. The pattern of the wallpaper faded beyond appreciation.

Delicate little fingers with beautifully manicured nails, tenderly, gently sealed a small brown padded packet and, using an antique fountain pen found in a junk shop nearby, wrote a single sentence on the front, dead centre. With a shrug of relief, the package was held aloft, like an offering to a god. Offered for the handiwork to be admired in the light of the fading day. This little packet of truth, full of woe, a tiny bombshell made of paper and sticky tape, was kissed softly, but just firmly enough to leave behind a trace of ruby red lipstick. The young man with long straight bleach blond hair reaching almost down to his waist, knew that his work was now complete, and his brown paper package, all tied up with string, was ready to do its job.

'I've done it, Daddy. Just like you asked me to,' he whispered into the air as he stepped lightly, joyfully, towards the door to send it on its way.

CHAPTER THREE

'Why's *she* here?'

Commissioner Grace Williams darted the briefest of glances at the nearest of the police frogmen who'd posed the question. She was no stranger to such open discourtesy. She wasn't there to be liked. The diver turned away abruptly, scanning the horizon purposefully to escape her gaze. He knew she would remember his face. There would be a price to pay.

The chauffeur-driven pristine black BMW had repeatedly tried and failed to dodge the potholes in the road leading up to the edge of Madryn Quarry. It had pulled up a few yards from the untidy gathering of exhausted police officers and rescue vehicles, their equipment discarded on the ground. A plastic tent had been erected to one side. She had to walk the last part on foot. The senior officer met her half way.

'What are we dealing with? A suicide?' She spoke without exchanging formalities.

'You've not been briefed then, Commissioner?' Her face cocked to one side, to make it clear she had not. An hour ago, she was in a high-level budget meeting in Bangor, discussing job cuts and other ways to 'streamline' the force. The message from ops had been garbled, but its essential meaning was clear enough – she was to get to Madryn PDQ. The message was shorn of pleasantries, and she hadn't stopped to question it. As Commissioner, her presence was unnecessary. Occasionally the powers that be decided otherwise. This was one such time.

She maintained an expression of benign condescension, but her slightly tightening features gave a clear sign that she was expecting to be filled in as a matter of urgency.

'Body. Male.' There was nothing unusual in this. Madryn was a favourite for thrill-seeking divers. A dozen or more had been lost to its depths in the last ten years. Likewise, it was a final haven for no-hopers, for those who could no longer see the point to this world. As she stepped tentatively towards the lip of the chasm, she thought, this was surely one more to add to the list. How many times had she stood on this spot? As a child, as an officer, and now as Commissioner. As kids they had imagined that the quarry was speaking. An anguished howling voice. Always angry. But it was just the wind. And as an officer, it still chilled her to the bone to look into its depths.

'Looks like the body's been down there some time, ma'am.' DCI Jack Watson had come to stand by her side. They went way back. Both had forgotten exactly how far. Maybe to their first days in the force.

'Exactly how long is "some" time?'

'Rough guess, about 20 years.'

'That's a very specific "rough guess."'

'We did have a little help, Commissioner. The body was well wrapped, well preserved. As was the ID in the pockets.'

Grace was struggling to understand why she had been brought to the quarry for what seemed to be an open and shut case. If they had ID, then what was the mystery? Surely just a solution to a cold case?

'And I was called out of an important meeting for what reason?' She glanced at her watch, and then over her shoulder at her car which had somehow manoeuvred for a quick getaway. She didn't have time to waste on a jumper.

'There was a driving licence in a wallet.' The officer seemed to be struggling with what he had to say next.

'It's in the name of Griffin. Tom Griffin. Of course, we'll have to wait for a proper ID, but...'

Grace had already turned before he had finished his sentence and was walking back to the car, tapping a speed dial number on her phone and holding it to her ear. Her call was answered almost immediately.

'It's me. I think we may have a problem. Actually, it's the mother of all fucking problems.' She ended the call and got back into the car, which started picking its way back along the track, skidding onto the main road, before picking up speed.

'Tom Griffin?' she mumbled to herself. 'That's just not possible.' Her driver, Gethin, looked in the rear-view mirror to assess if her words were meant for him. They clearly were not.

Grace scanned the horizon. There was a flash of light. A reflection maybe. On the hillside above. Someone was watching. Weren't they always?

CHAPTER FOUR

'Sitting ducks is what we are.' Sam opened the door slightly to the faint Afghan breeze, letting his right leg loll out of the cab.

'Let the good times roll!' The lead mastiff was ready to lead the convoy out of the compound. Midnight. Camp Bastion. FOB Eddy maybe 20 hours away? There was a nervous chuckle over the comms as the gates were swung open, and the pitch blackness of the wide Afghan countryside lay like a wound beyond.

'Let's get this show on the road.'

This show was 45 tonnes of fuel, kit and rations, everything the battle group needed. This convoy was 200 souls in a 500 metre train along Highway One, savouring the tarmac before it gave way to indistinct tracks through the wadis of the Afghan desert. 80 K to destination. Darkness, then dust, dusk and then mud. Leaving behind tents with air con for hours of uncertainty and ever-present danger from IEDs.

'Halt, halt, halt.' Dawn revealing Delta 8 ahead was mired in a churned-up wadi and the reccy-mecs were called forward to get them moving again. Through the corner of his eye Sam noticed a reflection – the crafty mirrors of the Talibob, signalling ahead to give their position, giving them ample time to plant IEDs along their path. Benno was rabbiting on about some nonsense back at Bastion. Some girl he met in the Pizza Hut. Gagging for it, he reckoned. The major up ahead was warning over the comms to be on their guard; keep their eyes peeled for Afghan natives up to no good. The dust was settling. He could see they were sitting in some shitty sandy bunker.

'Couple of nasty buggers over there. See that patch of scrub, left of that compound?' A warning flare rose like a Guy Fawkes rocket towards them, startling an 'insurgent' who let go of an old wooden wheelbarrow, and legged it back to safety.

An Apache helicopter appeared suddenly overhead, seeming to come from nowhere, and was gone just as quickly.

'Lucky fuckers in their first-class air-conned cockpits, probably supping a G&T!' Benno was scoping the horizon. The comms crackled into life again, 'Move on'.

Fort Edinburgh was still five miles distant, but a world away. Sam's mind was wandering to safer times and places, making a mental note to savour an ice cream next time he found himself on Llandudno pier, cursing the gulls.

All stop. The groan of the engines was punctuated by a distant explosion. 'Shit.' Benno lifted his feet off the dash and opened the truck door again to look back. 'Little fuckers, like a game of cat 'n' mouse.' It seemed an eternity before news came. 'All clear, no injuries, move on. Eddy's second star to the right and straight on till morning! Observe your arcs!'

'Too bloody right I will,' thought Sam, his hands gripping the wheel, praying the Op Barma guys had done their job seeking out the improvised explosive devices.

'Hey, check this out.' Benno had opened the window again, the dust billowing in.

'What the fuck are you playing at?'

'See there, ahead, to the left.'

The dust settled slowly and, in this dream, for it must have been a dream, because all this happened years ago... Sam focused on a man, in light coloured clothing, a heavy overcoat? He was standing in the desert all alone and watching the convoy go by. He's raising a hand as if to wave in recognition.

'But that's...' In the haze of uncertain reverie, in this half-remembered dream world, where facts seem just ever so slightly beyond reach, the name of the man in the camel-haired coat standing incongruously in the dust and haze of an Afghan field is lost to Sam. Maybe it was never found.

'He's a bad man if ever I saw one,' Benno was laughing again. Sam looked back in the mirror, he could see there was no one there.

'Best keep right on till morning then!' Benno laughed as his last moments flowed away. Sam knew all this. What he was seeing was history. Surely?

CHAPTER FIVE

'We used to come here as kids. Dad would buy us a milkshake. Strawberry. Maybe a Lucky Bag.'

Grace was taking in the interior of the Oceans Café on the pier. Like the rest of Llandudno, it had seen better days, but somehow always managed to reinvent itself. Its curious hexagonal space was packed with out-of-place modern blond wood tables and chairs. Far more than were ever needed other than on the wettest of summer days. The counter over-stocked with chocolate bars, charity collection tins for Help for Heroes, St David's Hospice and the RNLI.

'It can't have changed one bit.' She didn't mean it. She just wanted to fill the space with sound. Anything. Leon Vicary had said nothing since they'd met on Happy Valley Road, at the gates to the pier itself. Eyes obscured as always with dark glasses. She wondered whether she had ever seen his eyes. They had walked arm in arm along the pier towards the café.

They'd chosen to sit away from the door, but the café was deserted apart from the woman behind the counter, and an older man who drifted in and out of a back room. He seemed to have no purpose, other than to keep the lady at the counter company. She seemed disinterested.

Vicary tipped three measures from the sugar dispenser into his espresso cup, stirring relentlessly, eventually placing the spoon at right angles to the saucer. He raised the cup falteringly towards his lips which were puckering in readiness well in advance of the cup's arrival.

'You look like shit.' He seemed smaller than Grace had remembered. He had always been a great bear of a man, with a preference for long camel-haired coats and homburg hats that made him look for all the world like a wartime spiv. A dodgy geezer. Albeit a very successful one. But right now, he was looking all of his seventy-seven years, and more, she thought.

'There are very few people I would let speak to me in that way, my dear Grace. Luckily you are one of them. It was a rough night.' His gravelly voice was craving a cigarette. He twitched a look over his shoulder, took in the no smoking signs and seemed to be weighing up whether he could get away with a sneaky drag. The face of the woman behind the counter, already contorted by the sugar usage, suggested that would not be the case.

'Joy police on duty as always.' He smiled weakly in her direction and she set about cleaning tables she had already cleaned once or even twice in the time they'd been sitting there. She was watching them. Purely for entertainment. No agenda. Taking in how they sat, how they talked in whispers, how they would stop abruptly if they thought they were being overheard. Her hearing aid began to whistle, and she commenced an apparently fruitless battle to silence it.

'Behind the counter, in that little room, there's a trap door. Did you know that Grace?'

'No, why should I?' She took his word for it, and watched a couple walk by with a small dog.

'It's where they threw the rubbish, where they pissed when it was too busy to walk to the public lavs,' Vicary grinned again at the woman at the counter who was still trying to control her hearing aid.

'Nice.' Grace tried not to picture her squatting over the trap door, 'When the tide was in, I hope?'

'Not always. But I suppose times change.' A man with a fishing rod was climbing over the barrier down to the old Manx Ferry jetty.

'This rough night. Was it business or pleasure?'

'Always business, my dear girl, always business.' Vicary took another tentative sip at the coffee and winced, reaching again for the glass sugar pourer on the table. 'You can't get a good cup of coffee this side of Manchester,' he said deliberately loudly just as the woman had brought the hearing aid under control. She scowled, and scuttled back to the safety of the counter, and then into the back room. Her male friend appeared briefly, cigarette in hand, and stared at them.

'So tell me, dearest Grace. What's all this about Tom Griffin?' The meeting had clearly been called to order. This was now business, thought Grace.

'Body, male, came to light in the Madryn Quarry. Well wrapped...' Grace's own years in the police had engrained a matter-of-fact machine-gun approach to delivering information. Facts. Devoid of colour or emotion. Start with the general, and keep focusing in on the detail.

Vicary finished her sentence, '... in a tarpaulin? Trussed like a turkey with green paracord?' His gaze was drifting beyond Grace, maybe even beyond the café. Perhaps not on any person or thing, but a distant memory.

'Near enough.' Grace was considering what Vicary had just said. How much did he know?

'They used paracord for parachutes in the war. I do believe they've even used it to make repairs in space. Very durable, and usually very reliable.'

Clearly he knew more than Grace could tell him. But then Vicary had always been well connected. He had countless sources in the police apart from her, probably half the force, certainly more than she would ever have. Sources who would tip him off, bring him up to speed. She had no illusions who was in charge here. She could pretend, but she'd soon be reminded of the pecking order.

'You've been told already.' She knew from experience it was far better to let Vicary reveal what he knew and where he had gleaned the information from in his own time. Force him, and he would clam up. But stay silent, compliant, and he would exhibit a delicious pleasure in spilling the beans, revealing exactly how much he knew, or maybe how much of what he knew he wanted her to know.

'We'll put that down to an educated guess, shall we?' He smiled, leaning forward on the table, bringing his hands together, almost like a child praying. Palms pressed dead centre of his face, pressing the blood away from the mid-point of his forehead. Grace fancied that his eyes were closed, but she couldn't tell behind the dark glasses.

It was one of those moments when she felt as though she had always known him. As a toddler she'd clung tightly to the woollen-stockinged, embrocated leg of her grandmother the day Vicary first came to visit, embarrassed by the attention he gave her. Always a gift. A chocolate bar or soft toy. Always a lingering heavy-handed stroking of her hair. 'Such a pretty little thing,' he'd say.

To her as a child he was 'that old man,' although at the time he must only have been in his forties, dressed in the light brown coat, holding his hat in both hands in front of him, who came to tea from time to time, who sat in the ticking-clock silence of the parlour, drinking from the best china.

'I can't stop the investigation, you know that.' She watched to see if this would provoke a response. She studied his face. He seemed very old. Almost clinging to life. This was it. His end would come in a pathetic, deserted seaside greasy spoon end-of-the-pier café, and that perhaps would solve everything. Close the door on a million wrongs. Everyone could move on.

'The press have got hold of the story, and are digging around. Do you have any idea what they will find out? Is there anything I need to know?' Each question was separate, expectedly unanswered, left hanging in the chilled air of the café, made colder suddenly by the arrival of a young couple, over-wrapped in affluent clothing, their sickly smiles broadcasting the newness of their love.

Mention of the press seemed to reanimate Vicary. He flicked a hand into the air as if attempting to swat a persistent fly.

'Let them dig, my dear. What damage can they do now?'

He looked lost again, but eventually turned his head to watch the new arrivals take up a seat on the opposite side of the café. They were seeking intimate solitude too. Both ordering what looked like identical hot chocolates, which they hugged between identically-mittened hands. As far as they were concerned, they were the only two people in the world. Vicary smiled briefly at the couple. He raised a hand to attract the waitress to bring another coffee, but his signal was ignored. His smile withered. He let his hand settle across the table, palm upwards. Grace met it with hers, and he closed his fingers around her hand gently. Her warmth was matched by his coldness.

'So tell me, my dear, how is little Rhiannon?'

'My beautiful daughter, would you believe, will be eighteen on Friday.'

Vicary looked over at the young couple again, perhaps a moment's regret flashing across his face.

'Such a pretty little thing, such a pretty little thing indeed. So clever.' Grace could feel the chill of his hand winning over the comparative warmth of hers. She wanted to take her hand back and warm it against her cup, like the lovers. But she knew he had no intention of letting go.

CHAPTER SIX

Eddie Lavelle was sitting low in the driver's seat of the Bentley. He'd pulled in as close to the pier as he could get in Happy Valley Road. It was actually an access to a lock-up garage close to the Grand. Vicary owned it, like most things around this area, so there was little or no chance of someone trying to move him on.

It offered a commanding view. Not just along to the pier, but also eastwards towards the broad sweep of the bay – an arc of landladied bed and breakfast establishments, most of which had seen much better days. Craig-y-Don paddling pool, with the Little Orme behind. Tidily demarcated. A mass of people corralled into a pen, ripe for exploitation.

In the winter there were slim pickings. It was peopled by suspicious locals who could see trouble coming a mile away. Summers were a different matter. That's when you had the hordes of kiss-me-quick tourists who'd checked their common senses in at the border with Wales. Complicit. Looking for fun and adventure. Beginning their annual holiday week in hope, and ending it with dreams unfulfilled but with enough desire to want to come back and try again.

Gaggles of older women seeking a second or third chance at love, targeted by the charlies in boaters, who'd soft-soap them for a drink or a meal. They'd soon get wise to their tactics and graduate to hunting during the evening entertainment in some of the hotels. Fantasise about the performers, the tribute acts, the waiters, or seemingly single men, who often turned out to be 'recently bereaved' or 'coming to terms with their sexuality' after a lengthy but loveless marriage. By the end of the week, these ever-hopefuls would end up in the amusement arcades pushing tokens into slots, or trawling the charity shops for bargains.

There were hen parties but they largely looked after themselves. Little self-contained bundles of chaos. It was always hard to know whether the members of the groups were actually enjoying themselves, or whether it was simply a rite of passage that needed to be done. The leaders, the led, the led astray, the determinedly straying – somehow all bound together despite the mediocrity that surrounded them. Possibly corporeally too timid actually to do something memorable or amazing. Maybe that's where the alcohol came in. Helps you forget that nothing of note happened.

The ones that interested Eddie Lavelle the most were what he liked to call 'business tourists.' There were rich pickings for the gangs of Liverpool and Manchester. Some were clearly actually on holiday. Even crooks need some R & R sometimes. They weren't the problem. It was the organised gangs that he didn't like. And his boss, Mr Vicary, certainly didn't like them either. Muscling in on his patch. He was quite capable of servicing the increased demand for drugs, sex and gambling that came with the better weather. Plus, all the ancillary services such as ice cream and donkey rides. He didn't need any Scouse chancers creaming off his profits. It didn't sit with his business model.

So Eddie Lavelle was always watching. Watching the ebb and flow of tourists. They all moved in the same way. Predictably. It was the unpredictable ones that interested him most. Those who looked out of place. Or weren't moving in quite the way he would have expected. The ones who watched, trying to suss out the scam before making a move. And if they did? Then he'd lift them and show them some of the sights of Llandudno that were not on the tourist track. Just to scare them. Maybe strap them to the struts under the pier. Where the Manx Ferry used to dock. Under where the anglers usually hung out. So long as you worked out the height of the tides, it was usually enough to 'correct' their way of thinking. Of course, Eddie got it wrong sometimes, usually when he forgot to take into account unusually high tides. But usually he was spot on. Let them go the next morning and they'd scurry off back to their own patches.

It was reciprocal of course. He was always careful when he went to Liverpool or Manchester. He'd always try to dress down. Go easy on the gold. Use a less showy car. The Bentley was a bit obvious. In Manchester it was more of a problem. That was where he, and Vicary, had come from. They were too well known by the older, more established gangs. But equally the gangs assumed that they knew the rules and that they would be foolish to break them. A case of 'I see you, and I know you can see me, let's leave it at that.'

It was beginning to spit with rain. Vicary and Grace had been in the Oceans Café for about an hour. That was long even for them. Even though he had a soft spot for her, had steered her career, and probably still did. Both had a shared efficiency. Neither were fans of small talk. If there was something to be done, discuss it, get a plan, and carry it out.

In the distance, Eddie could make out two figures leaving the café. There was a polite embrace, some more words exchanged. Grace started walking back along the boardwalk of the pier alone. Vicary remained where he was. Stock still. Watching Grace walk away and back towards North Parade and Mostyn Street. Her car must have been parked somewhere near the shops.

Eventually Vicary began to walk, so slowly, almost reluctantly along the length of the pier. Eddie started the engine and let it idle for a short time to warm up the car. He drove the Bentley down to the entrance of the pier, at precisely the exact moment that Leon Vicary needed it. Eddie was proud of his timing.

Vicary opened the rear door and climbed in. He sat silently.

'West Shore?' Eddie looked back at Vicary in the rear-view mirror. Silence again. Eventually Vicary seemed to gather his thoughts.

'Home, Boss?'

'No, not yet.' Vicary removed his dark glasses and pinched the bridge of his nose. He was feeling so tired. More than just physically. It felt like he was being drawn down by ropes attached to his arms, legs, chest, shoulders. Hell is getting impatient, he thought.

'Anywhere in particular, Mr Vicary?'

'Otherworld, Eddie. I need to check on my investment.'

Femi Kayode is the Creative Director of an advertising agency in Namibia. He holds a Master's in Clinical Psychology, dabbles in Futures Studies and writes soapies on the side. He lives in Windhoek with his family and two hyperactive dogs.

femi.kayode@gmail.com

A Certain Beauty

A past not too distant

The October sun is as hot as the blood of the angry mob. John Paul follows the crowd as they chant and push the three young men pleading for mercy. Soon, they are stripped naked, their scrotums shrunken from fear as the beating continues with the chanting as an incongruous soundtrack. Sticks. Stones. Bricks. Iron. Bones break, blood flows. The tearing of flesh draws short-lived screams from lungs too weak to sustain any sound longer or stronger than brief outbursts of agony. The men fall but are swiftly pulled up and dragged through the streets, towards a place no one picked out, but everyone seems to know.

It had rained the day before, making the red earth muddy in places where trees shaded the ground, and the sun had not dried all the rainwater. The young men fall and become covered in mud as their blood mixes with the brown earth. It is here the crowd stops moving, and where John Paul takes a spot that gives him the best vantage point of the young men who are now properly cornered like animals in pen.

It would have been quicker to strike a death blow to each one, without the suffering, the chanting, and the beating. But the demon that unites the crowd does not want quick. By the time tyres are thrown over the heads of the young men like oversized necklaces, and the smell of petrol wafts so strong that some in the crowd cover their noses, madness has staked its claim on what is left of the day. Just as the strike of a match births a solitary flame, one of the young men draws his last breath as a brick crushes his skull. The remaining two scream, as fire licks skin and hair.

John Paul lowers his smartphone and looks around. His phone is not the only one bearing digital witness to flesh melting off braying men as they try to stand and run from eager flames, while the crowd cheers their inevitable failure. The phone's battery is low, signalling the right time to leave. It's over anyway. By tomorrow, the young men will be stiff and charred, burnt so crisply, there will be no stench of rotting flesh in the humid air. Their remains will be here for a couple of days at least, on exhibition to remind and warn. But I know John Paul won't be back. Death does not interest him. Dying, on the other hand, is different. As he walks away from the still chanting crowd and the burning young men, I also know he's not happy that his target had died too soon. I follow him in the shadows, unable to unsee the nightmare behind us.

He does not look back, so neither can I.

PART ONE—SIX DEGREES (PRESENT DAY)
1—*The why, not the what*

Unless I'm mistaken, a riot is about to break out in the departure lounge of the Lagos Domestic Airport. When it comes to crowds and understanding how they think, I am not always wrong.

'It's been three hours! Someone should at least tell us what is going on!'

Spit sprays out of the irate passenger's mouth, as he barks into the face of the unconcerned airline staff.

Good luck with that, I think from my vantage point where I sit with my meat pie and Coca-Cola. I am at a table in the Mr Bigg's restaurant facing the check-in counter of Okada Airlines. I have deliberately chosen my position so that if the delayed airplane does appear, I will know and not be left behind when it decides to fly to Port Harcourt. Unlikely as that possibility seems after three hours of no news.

'Sir, the flight is delayed. I've told you this over and over—'

'What is delaying it?' the passenger barks out in derision.

You're lucky he is even answering you after that spray of mucus, electrolytes and water you just downloaded on him. I know I am being unkind. But after reading my copious notes on the Okriki Three and doubting the wisdom of taking this assignment for the one-billionth time, I'm not feeling charitable towards either my fellow passengers or the Okada Airlines staff.

'I can't answer that, ma. All I know is that the flight is delayed and if you'll be patient—'

'For how long?' The agonised question is from a short, amply figured, sweaty passenger who has no right to be this frustrated, considering I saw her come through the checkpoint less than 30 minutes before the flight was supposed to have departed. If there was any sanity at the Lagos Domestic Airport, the woman should have missed the flight. 'We've been waiting for...'

Three hours. I complete in my head. But if you count how long since the Uber dropped me at the airport, it would be five hours. Then again, the other passengers are not running from their homes to avoid a confrontation with their cheating spouse. OK. *Probably* cheating spouse. To be fair, I know the hurried way I packed my bags and left home in the early hours of this morning had everything to do with the fact that I was not willing to ask my wife the question that was uppermost in my mind.

Are you having an affair?

It had taken enormous willpower to swallow that question this morning as she stood in our bedroom, arms akimbo, pacing back and forth, as I walked around her from our wardrobe to the open suitcase on the bed. She had on a light cotton housecoat, wrapped around her slim frame. Even in my haste to get away from her, my wife's beauty still made me catch my breath. Her long braids were pulled back from her beautiful dark face, so there was no masking her disapproval as she watched me pack.

'You're really doing this?'

I grunted out a yes as I made a show of counting the number of underpants I was packing while simultaneously avoiding her eyes.

'And it doesn't matter that I think it's a really bad idea?'

Seven would be overkill. Surely, they would have laundry service at the hotel. I reduced the number of underwear I was putting into the suitcase. I didn't look at my wife when I responded in what I hoped was a carefully crafted neutral voice.

'We've been through this, Folake.'

'You're not a detective, Philip.'

'As you keep telling me. Your faith inspires and motivates.'

'Don't you dare play that card! Not after all we've been through. No one, not one, has shown more faith in you than I have.'

'You reckon now is the best time to stop?'

'You can't leave your family to go off to some village to solve a case that's been cold for almost three years and expect me to throw a send-off party!'

I straightened up from the open suitcase and faced her, making *eye contact*. I did this to get her to lower her voice and give the impression that we were having a *conversation*. That I was *engaged* and *listening* to her. I knew if I continued my passive aggressive stance, she would likely blow up and shout the house down just to get some reaction from me. Folake blowing up is not a pretty sight, and at six-thirty in the morning, I was not going to unleash my wife's rage on the children.

'I'm not solving anything. I am just going to find out why what happened did happen.'

'How is that not solving a case?' she snorted.

'Because there's nothing to solve. Everyone knows what happened. And if they don't, they can find out on a thousand websites online. But no one knows why it happened.'

'I've never understood the logic of understanding why a murder happened. Even in your days at the SFPD. Surely you can't understand *why* something happened without knowing what happened?'

If I had gone into an explanation of my work as an investigative psychologist, I wouldn't be waiting for the delayed flight now. Besides, Folake and I have had this discussion a number of times in the past two decades, ever since the days of supporting each other through our respective PhDs. She pretended to misunderstand my work when it suited her. Like this morning. So, instead of talking about the case, I tried to explain why I was taking it.

'This is a wonderful opportunity to put my skills to practice in the real world—'

'A real and dangerous world,' she cut in sharply.

I had no answer to that one. No doubt travelling to Okriki might be considered dangerous for someone like me, who had lived the better part of his adult life in the United States, but it would still have been nice to hear my wife say: 'Go, honey. If anyone can find out what led to the mobbing, beating and burning to death of three young undergraduates, you're the one. You've got this honey—'

'It's a foolhardy scheme, and you know it! I don't know what you are trying to prove here.'

I moved around the clothes in the suitcase from left to right and back again so that when I answered her, I hoped my voice did not betray my rising anger.

'I'm trying to prove that I'm more than a two-bit lecturer without tenure, that I have skills that can be applied in the real world, right here in Nigeria.'

'Going off to some village to solve multiple murders is not going to get you tenure,' she spat out.

But it will get me away from you. It will take my mind away from the sad, desperate possibility that you are cheating on me. Of course, I didn't say any of this out loud. I hate fighting. Especially fighting that involved shouting. Besides, when it comes to a war of words, few can beat Professor Afolake Taiwo. I know this first hand because, in seventeen years of marriage, I have rarely won an argument with my wife. She is a professional arguer, being a lawyer and the youngest Professor of Law at the University of Lagos. She is that good.

Which is why I didn't want to continue the discussion. The possibility of her being right made me pack faster. I could feel her eyes on me – gauging me, wondering what other tactics to employ. I know her well enough virtually to see the gears of her sharp mind changing.

'OK, Philip. Let's say you get there and you stumble on what really happened, on why it happened. What do you want to do with it? Write a book?'

I sighed and snapped my suitcase shut. I faced her squarely.

'We are not in the US, Folake. This is Nigeria. You don't chase after the gory details of multiple killings in the hope of writing the next bestseller.'

'Then in the name of everything holy, tell me what you're hoping for?'

'I hope to do exactly what I am being paid to do, what I was trained to do – ascertain how and why what happened came to happen. I told you. The father of one of the boys is paying me to—'

'Yes, yes we know.' She threw her hands in the air and rolled her eyes in exasperation. 'He wants you to write some report because he doesn't believe the conclusion of the police that his son was a common thief! But the facts are there – the boys were lynched and killed because they were caught stealing! It's all there on social media.'

'Have you seen it?'

Her instantaneous shudder was my answer.

'I have watched it a hundred times at least.' I continue, sparing her the agony of recounting what she saw on any of the several sites on which the Okriki Three killing was available. 'And you know what? The horror doesn't reduce. For something that's so obvious, you'd think the answers are clear. People can't be so crazy as to round up three boys and burn them in broad daylight just because they think they're thieves.'

She sat on the side of the bed.

'Nothing makes sense in this country,' she said.

The statement was as much an observation as a judgement.

'Everything makes sense when you know why people do what they do.'

'Psychobabble nonsense.' Even in her anger, she must have known she crossed the line. Her hand rose to cover her mouth as if she wanted to take back words that at once damned my person and my career path.

I bent to zip up the suitcase to mask my hurt, so that when I straightened and looked at her, my voice was steady and as neutral as when we started the conversation.

'Thank you. Now may I go and apply my psychobabble on a matter for which I am going to be handsomely rewarded? Excuse me.'

I lifted the suitcase off the bed and walked out with it, quickly, before she regained her wit. On this one occasion, I was determined to have the last word.

'This useless country. Only in Nigeria can someone take people's money and try this kind of nonsense!'

Another passenger's voice brings me back from my reverie. I don't wait to hear further. After the morning with Folake and my insecurities about this assignment, I have no motivation to coerce an explanation for the flight delay from the reluctant airline staff. I drown out the noise around me as I mentally give it another hour or so before irate passengers and rude airline ground crew exchange blows.

I now turn my attention to the one thing I was trained to understand. A crime scene.

2—*Check*

A crime scene can range from the perfectly orderly to the maddeningly chaotic.

The words of my old teacher and mentor, Professor Albert Cook, come to me every time I evaluate a crime scene: 'Death is messy Philip, but dying is a shithouse.' Prof, as I fondly called him, never subscribed to the idea that any crime scene fitted into a given set of typologies. He used to say: 'People fuck up, and that's where the clue to knowing what really happened lies. In life or death, the answer to everything lies in the fuck-up.'

I miss Prof. He was my PhD thesis supervisor at the University of Southern California, my first boss and the person who introduced me to the then evolving field of investigative psychology. Prof is retired now but remains active in 'butting into other people's shithouses' as he calls it. Perhaps I should send him the YouTube link to the murders. It would be interesting to hear what the old man thought of this particular shithouse.

I look at my notes.

Crime scene mos def not organised.

Although, when one considers how the crowd appear to be choreographed, how their rage seemed so focused on the three young men they were killing – murdering – at least some of the conditions of a staged crime scene could apply. Take the aggression directed at the victims before they were burnt. Classic premeditation. And the tyres. Surely, they couldn't have just appeared – someone, or a group of people, had to have gone out of their way to bring them to the scene. The crime scene, in this case, should be limited to where the boys were finally burnt and killed.

Personalisation of victim(s)

I keep drawing circles around 'personalisation'. Under normal circumstances, it is theoretically safe to assume a mob killing is not personal. But practically, given the intensity with which the young boys were attacked, it would make sense to assume some collective displacement. If the young men were suspected thieves, then the way they were attacked would imply that a critical number of the attackers had experienced some robbery before and the young men represented past robberies by others that went unpunished. But is that argument tenable for almost a hundred angry people? I place several question marks against 'personalisation' and write: *Get data on the rate of robberies in the neighbourhood over the past month leading to the killing.*

There are other indications of an organised crime scene – the demand for the victims to be submissive and the use of restraints at some point during the whole heart-breaking exercise were classic indicators – but this is where the staged crime scene typology ends.

In another section of my notebook, I've listed the characteristics of a disorganised crime scene, and I evaluate them now, as I nibble at my Mr Bigg's meat pie. I look up to see whether any one of the frustrated passengers has resorted to violence. Not yet.

Bodies left at the scene of the crime. Check.

Bodies left in full view for anyone to see. Check.

Depersonalisation of victims. Check.

I doodle around this sentence. Can one be sure? Is it possible that no one knew the boys? What about the person who claimed he was being robbed? I quickly write: *Interview alarm raiser.*

Minimal conversation. Check.

Spontaneity –

Reports had said the mob descended on the boys after an alarm was raised that they were robbing a resident of the town. There was no way over a hundred angry people were lying in wait to be summoned to participate in a necklace killing. So, check.

Unexpected and sudden violence to victims. Check.

I pause here. The human stories about a crime are as important as the crime scene itself. The motivations of the narrator (perpetrator, victim or witness) in telling the truth or a lie, can shed a considerable amount of light on what really happened.

I flip the pages of my notes to where I wrote: *Emeka Nwamadi.*

3—*A grieving father*

'I've heard a lot about you, Dr Taiwo.' His voice was deep, cultured and educated but his Igbo origins had been not completely erased, especially when he called out his full name.

'Chiemeka Nwamadi,' he said as he shook my hand.

'Good to meet you, Mr Nwamadi.'

'Emeka, please. Let's not stand on formalities.'

'Let's not stand at all. Come,' said Abubakar, who'd be my boss if my contract was permanent rather than that of a guest lecturer whose services are procured strictly upon the availability of budget.

He ushered – more like ordered – us to sit on the front row chairs that faced the desk from where I had just delivered one of my lectures on crowd control to the cadets at the Police College in Lagos. I like Abubakar.

He's old school – the 32nd Commandant of the Police College who still harbours illusions of restoring the glory days of the Nigerian Police Force.

As we made ourselves comfortable on the sturdy chairs, I couldn't shake the feeling that Nwamadi's name was familiar, and just before it began to bother me, Abubakar must have read my mind.

'Emeka is the MD of National Bank,' he said, and I mentally slapped my head. The man was the head of the country's third largest commercial bank. As soon as the recognition registered, another hazy detail hovered in the fringes of my mind and Abubakar came to the rescue again.

'I'm not sure if you know about the case of the Okriki Three,' he said.

Shock was my first reaction, then compassion. This was the father of one of the three boys lynched and burnt to death about two years ago at Okiriki. It was all over the news, and this man's fight, along with the other parents', to bring the people who killed their sons to some kind of justice was the stuff of headlines many months ago. I understood then why Emeka's eyes looked like a barely contained dam.

'I am so sorry, sir.' It was the best I could offer.

Chiemeka Nwamadi nodded, almost sympathetically, like a grotesquely deformed person pities your guilt for staring.

'This is why we are here, Philip. You know what haffened. Everyone knows what haffened.' When Abubakar is excited, his Hausa heritage betrays him and his *p*'s turn to *f*'s.

Actually, I didn't know what happened. Not at that first meeting. I had an idea, but, frankly, the whole story was too sordid for me. My twin sons had just turned sixteen and it was not hard to picture them in university, away from home and finding themselves in the wrong place at the wrong time, like the Okiriki Three. It was self-preservation that prevented me from knowing more.

'I'm not sure where I come in, sir?' I responded.

'Tell him.' Abubakar nodded at Emeka.

But Emeka did not speak immediately. Rather he reached into his leather briefcase, which I had assumed carried a laptop, and brought out two well-bound documents. He put them on the table between us, but I already knew what they were. The first was my master's thesis, poetically titled: '*Strange Fruit: understanding the psychology of the crowds that lynched black people in the South*'. The second was my PhD thesis, a continuation of sorts titled: '*Strange Harvest: how crowds commit murder.*' From the way the documents were bound, it was clear they were not bought in any bookstore, most probably downloaded from the online library of the University of Southern California where I researched and wrote both theses.

I looked at Abubakar questioningly. He was one of the few people who knew the existence of the studies. I had presented them as part of my résumé when I applied to the Police College. Abubakar shrugged and waved at Emeka to speak.

Emeka looked at me intently and said, 'There's a lot of stories about what happened in Okriki the day my son was killed. I don't believe any of them, so I'm here to ask you to help me find out what really happened.' He stressed the 'really' part of the sentence in that way I was used to hearing and to which I had my standard response.

'No, sir. You mustn't mistake me for a detective. I am a psychologist with expertise in studying crime scenes to understand the motives behind a crime and how it was committed. Most of my investigations are purely an exercise in academic exploration.' It was a speech well-rehearsed from years of rejecting being labelled as something I know I am not and do not wish to be. I am not a detective, and even when I worked in the US after a PhD in investigative psychology, it was always a battle trying to explain the limits of my expertise to my San Francisco Police Department colleagues.

'I read these books.'

'They're academic papers.'

'Brilliant in my opinion,' Emeka responded as he tapped well-manicured fingers on the bulk of bound papers. 'I did my MBA at the University of Austin and your subject matter is not new to me. But I've never read anything like your analysis of crowd behaviour.'

'They are post-event observations. Not forensic in nature.'

'But insightful nonetheless,' Emeka insisted.

'I told you he is humble,' Abubakar said to Emeka, sounding like my agent. He turned to me. 'Phirif...,' when Abubakar's *l*'s turn to *r*'s, his Hausa Police Boss mode is in full bloom, '... you're the only one that can feece together what haffened. These feeful need your herf. As the only investigative psychologist in this country—'

'That you know of,' I interrupted.

Abubakar waved his hand dismissively. 'If I don't know them, they don't exist. You, I know. And I know you can herf diz feeful.'

I wanted to respond that I was happy being a lecturer. If there was anything I learnt from those soul-numbing eight and a half years of 'piecing together' the motives and modus operandi of some of the most horrendous crimes known to man, it was that there are no winners in any crime involving the loss of life. Definitely not the victims, the perpetrators, or even the investigators. I was about to voice a more determined refusal when Emeka broke into my thoughts.

'Have you watched the video, Dr Taiwo?' he asked.

'Please. Call me Philip.' I hate being called 'doctor'. I think it's pretentious, given my area of expertise.

'Philip.' Nwamadi conceded without missing a beat. 'Have you watched it? The video?'

I shook my head and Emeka reached for his slim smartphone. He pressed the screen twice and handed the phone to me with what seemed like a challenge in his eyes.

Seconds later, as the last minutes of Kevin Nwamadi's life played out on my palm, all thoughts of my wife's possible infidelity disappeared in the face of the horror that unfolded on the screen of the iPhone.

4—A beautiful stranger with an ominous warning

Red pill or blue pill. I consider the two options as I settle into my seat. The red pill will prevent nausea, a persistent and somewhat irritating reaction to the anxiety attacks I get during air travel. I stop short of calling it a fear of flying since I have racked up enough air miles in my life to know the condition is nowhere near debilitating. The blue pill, a lightweight diazepam, will control the anxiety and put me to sleep but won't prevent dreams of fire and young men pleading for mercy.

'Ladies and gentlemen, welcome to Flight 2435 going to Port Harcourt. We would like to apologise for the delay of this flight.'

I snort at this. One would think the delay was an hour at most. And I had been right in my reading of the crowd at the airport. Some of the passengers did get violent, and only the announcement that the plane would in fact fly had prevented the pummelling of rude airline staff at the departure hall less than two hours ago. Total waiting time: five hours, twenty-seven minutes.

'Captain Duke and the crew will do our best to arrive in Port Harcourt with your safety and comfort as our primary goal.'

Perhaps I shouldn't take any pill. It's fifty-five minutes to Port Harcourt. I should be able to hold out for an hour.

'Please settle down as the plane refuels and we will be on our way.'

Refuelling is no joke. Being told an aeroplane is refuelling at an airport runway in Lagos creates visions of a petrol tanker wading through heavy traffic and waiting in long queues to purchase petrol at whatever is the prevailing price of the day, then crawling back through even more dense traffic to offload the fuel onto the waiting plane. Of course, logic dictates that aviation fuel is not the same as what goes into my four-year-old Toyota Prado. Nevertheless, it's best to put both pills away until I'm sure this plane will actually leave the airport.

Just then, the passenger in the adjoining seat arrives and immediately I decide: no pill, red or blue, throughout this flight. The beautiful woman standing over me is worth the sacrifice. Her face is so perfectly made up that my mind conjures precision-engineered mechanical robots applying lipstick and eyeliner. Her waist is squeezed into a form-fitting dress which accentuates her full figure as she reaches to put away several bags into the overhead compartment. Her leather laptop bag will not go in, so she sits, puts it under the seat in front of her and turns to me with a thousand-megawatt smile.

'Hi,' she says.

'Hello,' I almost choke out my reply. She is that gorgeous.

'I was afraid I'd be late.' She says as she unnecessarily smooths her dress and settles back on the seat.

'Everyone's late. The flight was delayed.'

'I know. As soon as my queue boy told me, I just took my time. When these flights are delayed, it's not a joke.'

'Queue boy?'

She looks at me squarely then and raises an expertly traced eyebrow. 'Someone you hire to stand in the queue for you.'

She smiles like she can see the inside of my head trying to wrap itself around the concept. 'These flights will always be late. So, you pay someone to come ahead of you to stand in the queue. They call you as soon as boarding starts.'

'But the traffic. Surely there is no way you can make it between the first call and the final boarding call.'

She laughs. A gay laugh that tinkles loud enough to get the attention of everyone close by. Overweight women throw daggers with their eyes as they place her squarely in the husband-snatcher box. If any of them had my wife's number, her phone would be ringing this second. *What are you doing there?* They would scream. *You leave your husband to travel alone to Port Harcourt? Are you crazy? Get here now and come and save him from witchcraft parading in Chanel No 5 perfume.* Meanwhile, the men look like they would all trade places with me in a Lagos bus stop minute.

'Which is why I'm the last to get on the flight.'

It's my turn to laugh. I stretch out my hand, 'Philip Taiwo. Pleasure to meet you.'

Ringed fingers take my hand. 'Salome Briggs. Likewise.'

Roe Lane lives in London and works at RADA. She has worked in theatre for a decade as playwright, director, script reader, teacher, and librarian. She grew up in the UK, Nepal, and Malawi. Her favourite crime writers include Jasper Fforde, Robin Stevens, Ruth Rendell and Agatha Christie.

roe@roelane.co.uk

Unfinished Business

She ate three mouthfuls of birthday cake and then froze, dropping her fork with a clatter. The familiar itching of her mouth and throat was followed far too quickly by the prickly swelling of her lips and tongue. She lurched up from the table, knocking a champagne flute and catching the hem of her dress under a chair leg. The six others around the table fell silent and then rapidly grew loud as she stumbled, dizzy and nauseous, across the room. She flung open the door but stopped halfway down the hall and vomited, supported by someone – maybe a few people, she didn't notice who – that had followed her from the table.

She didn't stop for long: the terror of the worst allergic reaction of her life carried her up the staircase to her room. Someone overtook her and opened the bedroom door. She was starting to see spots but followed, her lungs protesting. A hand picked up her backpack, and she reached for it, scrabbling through the contents to find the pouch where she kept her EpiPen. The spots were larger now, obscuring her vision with dizzy whirls, but she found it by touch. A hand took it from her. With relief, she heard the zip opening, but as she was waiting for the reassuring stab to the thigh, she began to lose consciousness.

Her final thought before she collapsed was to try to fall on her back, rather than forwards onto her swollen pregnant belly.

When she resurfaced, she was sitting in a hard seat. Everything was so bright that she immediately closed her eyes. She tried to move or speak but nothing happened. Her body seemed to take ages to catch up with her mind – or was it the other way around?

Eventually, she felt more than the seat beneath her. She felt her neck ache, as her body was slumped backwards over the chair, her arms by her sides. She felt something clutched in her hand. Something dry and flimsy. Paper?

She inched her heavy head to upright, then opened her eyes again slightly. Over what seemed like hours, she managed to open them fully and focus on the slip of blue paper in her hand. It had three black marks on it. She recognised them – she was sure she recognised them.

Her brain was working so slowly.

The first one was a straight vertical line. She knew that line.

'One!' It was her voice: she heard it and felt it come out of her mouth before her mind realised she was going to speak. The first symbol was a one. And the second – an oval – that was a zero. But the third was difficult. What was that curly squiggle? Her finger traced it several times as her brain tried to decipher it.

'One zero eight,' said a voice. It wasn't hers this time. But it was right – the squiggle was an eight! She looked up at a painfully bright room with benches in rows, a glass-fronted counter, and a floor of institutional green.

'One zero eight,' said the voice again, and she saw the number flash up above the counter. Her brain was rushing now, hurtling towards real time to catch up with her body.

'One zero eight!' she croaked, managing to stand. 'That's me!'

She walked across the room, remembering as she did so that the last time she had been standing, back in the bedroom, she had been unable to do more than stagger. Why did she feel so oddly light? And strange? It felt as if something was missing, but her brain couldn't fit the pieces together to make any sense.

As she neared the counter, she frowned. She'd been to A&E before with her allergy, once even in an ambulance, but she hadn't had to sit in the waiting room that time – she'd been rushed through on a stretcher. What were they playing at here? Surely this was worse than last time? Why weren't the doctors running around with adrenaline and oxygen? Why had she been left alone in the waiting room clutching a numbered ticket? Where were the paramedics who brought her here? And where were her friends?

'Hello there. Can I have your name, please?' said the face behind the counter.

'Never mind that – I've had a severe allergic reaction – you need to help me!' Her voice slowed as she spoke. How could she speak if her airways had closed up?

'Your name, please?'

She looked closer at the man behind the counter. He seemed old – much too old to be working at an NHS reception. He looked shrivelled and bony in his overlarge grey scrubs.

'Um... Polly Tang,' she said, and the man nodded, before getting up and opening a filing cabinet on the wall behind him.

'Date of birth?' he asked.

'Twentieth of February 1985,' she replied, and the man drew out a large manila folder.

'And it was an allergic reaction, you said?' he asked, sitting down again and leafing through the folder at a desk that Polly was puzzled to see had no computer on it. 'Could you be more specific?'

'Nuts. Cashew nuts. They must have been in the cheesecake.'

'And that was today? The tenth?'

'Well, yes!'

The man nodded and made a note in the folder. 'And can you tell me where the death took place?'

'The... what? I'm sorry? What did you say?'

'Your death – where did it happen?'

'But I'm not... well obviously I'm not dead! A&E is really not an appropriate place to make sick jokes like that!' She heard her voice get loud and shrill and felt a shiver scuttle up her spine.

'A&E?' the man looked up at her and put his pen down. 'This isn't A&E. I'm sorry.' He stood up. 'I'm afraid you did not survive this allergic reaction, Miss Tang. This is not a hospital; it is the waiting room for the afterlife. This is where deaths are officially recorded.'

'What?' Polly whispered. She looked around her. The waiting room stretched off into the distance, infinite rows of wooden benches facing infinite glass-fronted counters. And on every bench sat someone looking just as distressed as she felt. The old man at the next counter to her was the same shade of grey-yellow as the hospital gown he was wearing, and beyond him was a girl covered in bloodstains, one leg jaggedly severed at the knee. Hanging above Polly's head was a large sign saying, 'Death Administration Office: Reception', and on the counter was a brass plaque proclaiming the man behind it to be 'Aeacus: *Death Administrator*'.

Polly gave a choked sob. 'No,' she whimpered.

'I am sorry, Miss Tang,' said Aeacus. 'I understand how hard it is. We do offer therapy sessions to help you process this, but I must get your information entered here first, so you can proceed to your new home.'

'No! I don't want to. I want to go back! I'm not dead – I'm better – the EpiPen must have worked!'

Aeacus sighed. 'Have a look in the mirror, Miss Tang.'

Polly took a step to her left and looked into a mirror that she hadn't noticed before, hanging beside the counter. She screamed as her brain finally caught up with her body, shocked awake by the image looking back at her.

Her Queen of Hearts costume had been cut down the middle from neckline to hem, revealing her underwear. The heart-shaped collar framed her neck, which had been punctured: a clinical tube was jabbed into her throat. But it didn't hurt.

Her hair was flecked with vomit, and her face was swollen and blue. And right across her abdomen was a deep slash like a large angry mouth, wet with blood. But that didn't hurt either and, while it was bloody, it wasn't actually bleeding. She looked back up at her swollen face. Her lips were grey, her cheeks waxy and her eyes unblinking.

She hadn't blinked since she'd opened her eyes, Polly realised. And she hadn't breathed once.

She looked back at Aeacus. He wasn't blinking either. But instead of acknowledging her death – because of course she was dead, it explained everything – she said, 'Where the fuck is my baby?'

Aeacus sighed again. 'I don't know.'

'Well, he's been ripped out of me way before his due date, and I'm now dead, so did he die too? Is he here somewhere?' Polly looked behind her, searching through the bewildered dead for her child.

'I don't know, Miss Tang. I will have to check with my counterparts at the Birth Administration Office, but I'll need that address.'

'I don't know the address! It was a holiday cottage: we rented it for Hayat's birthday party. It's called Shepherd's Rest. Somewhere in the Peak District, near Ashbourne. I don't know.' She burst into tears.

'Thank you, Miss Tang, if you would just wait a moment.' He pulled a ledger off a shelf and flicked through the pages. He made notes in the ledger, in the manila folder, and then on a card, so slowly that Polly clenched her fists in impatience. Then he creaked up from his chair and over to a candlestick telephone that stood on a shelf behind him. After a brief conversation, he came back to Polly.

'I'm pleased to say that your son survived an emergency caesarean section conducted just before you died and was taken to the Derby District Hospital.'

'Oh!' Relief hit Polly like a slap, and her knees buckled under her. She caught herself on the counter. As she lowered her arms, her hands went automatically to her belly and then recoiled in horror at its loose emptiness.

Aeacus was wearing a large signet ring, which he stamped onto an ink pad and then onto the card.

'Now, this is your death card,' he said, passing it through a hatch. 'You'll need to show it again at the other end.'

'The other end of what?'

'Your journey, Miss Tang. If you proceed through that door, you can catch the ferry—'

'Are you kidding me? You're telling me I'm dead, and you want me to calmly toddle off to the land of the dead without even seeing my baby?'

'If you have unfinished business, you are welcome to revisit anywhere you went during your lifetime. Providing your visits are conducted only at night, and that you complete a risk assessment before interacting with any living people. The full terms and conditions are in this brochure.'

'Only places I went to during my lifetime? But you just said my baby was in some hospital in Derby: I've never been there!'

'Well, who will receive custody of him in your absence?'

'Um... Nadim, I suppose. He's his father, but we've broken up.'

'And I take it you have visited his home?'

'Yes, but—'

'Good. Then, when he has been discharged, you will be able to visit him there.'

'But he's a premature baby – he might be kept in for ages! Or he might not... we don't even know if he'll survive. I have to see him now, in the hospital.'

'I'm afraid the usual procedure is to wait for him to be moved, or of course for him to arrive here.'

'Are you kidding me? You want me to hang around here waiting for my baby to die? That's the "usual procedure"? There had better be an unusual procedure I can follow.'

'Well, yes,' admitted Aeacus. 'You could try registering a request with the Appeals Office – but they rarely make an exception.'

'Right. And where is this Appeals Office?

'It's on the other side. And don't worry, Miss Tang,' Aeacus added, 'you'll get used to being dead. Everyone does.'

Polly opened the door and found herself on the bank of a large river, where a queue of people was waiting to climb aboard a row of paddle steamers bobbing on the water. She heard lots of different languages being spoken, and saw people wearing clothes she had never seen before. Most of the people around her looked as shell-shocked as she felt, but a few were relaxed, as if this was just a day out. Two old women were doing a crossword together.

Most people were on their own, but a few stood in huddles, supporting each other. A woman in a torn headscarf was holding hands with two bedraggled children, trying to be cheerful. Polly couldn't understand the language they were speaking, but when the mother started singing to her crying daughter, she felt tears well up in her own eyes. She was glad none of her friends had died too – of course she was – but looking at the drowned family comforting each other made her feel lonely.

She felt a tap on her shoulder and turned to see an old Chinese couple smiling at her. The old lady spoke to her, but Polly shook her head.

'Sorry – I don't speak Mandarin. Cantonese? *Gwóngdōngwá?*'

The woman's face fell. They smiled and shrugged at each other apologetically and the woman turned back to her husband, leaving Polly feeling even lonelier.

The queue diminished and Polly's turn came quickly. She and the old Chinese couple took the last seats on a boat which was immediately unhitched. As they drew away from the harbour, the woman at the helm raised an old-fashioned tin megaphone.

'Hello, and welcome aboard the *Tuonetar*. My name is Sharron, and I will be your captain today.'

'Yoh! A lady captain!' scoffed a middle-aged man with a South African accent. 'And not a bloody lifejacket anywhere. Lucky if we don't drown.' Polly rolled her eyes and caught the eye of a teenage boy opposite doing the same.

'This is crazy,' the boy muttered to two others either side of him. Polly thought they seemed familiar. They looked like they were in uniform: they all sported grey hoodies, long basketball shorts, and over-sized trainers. Their wounds matched too: all three had bloodstained holes in their chests.

'Yeah. I never been on a boat before,' replied the boy to his right, whose white skin was translucent with blood loss, 'but I guess it don't matter if I can't swim now, huh?' His friends snorted with laughter and attempted bravado, and Polly realised why she recognised them. Their smiling faces had flashed up on her phone's news app that morning, under the headline 'Shooter targets classmates in Californian middle school massacre'.

Remembering that gave her a pang of sadness: not for the three boys, selfishly, but for the friends she had just lost. She had set the news app to alert her with a dramatic 'dun-dun-DUN!' noise, like in a cheesy film. It had made her jump every time, which in turn had made Max laugh at her. It had happened three times in the car driving up from London.

'Dun-dun-DUN!'

'For fuck's sake, not again, you'll make me crash!' said Hayat, after Polly's jump and Max's snort of laughter. It was two o'clock on the Friday afternoon, lazy drizzle pattered the windscreen, and three voices singing along to Adele filled the car. Polly glanced at her phone, saw that the alert was just some non-news about Brexit, and swiped it away.

'You have reached your destination,' announced Hayat's phone, in a voice that brooked no arguments.

'Er... That's a field,' said Hayat. 'Please tell me we are not going fucking camping.'

'No,' said Polly, 'but they said Google Maps is not very accurate round here. Let's keep going...' The car crested a hill. 'There it is.'

'Woah!' said Max.

The house was set back from the road, with a driveway sweeping round it to the rear. It was tall, white, and imposing: three storeys of symmetrical Georgian windows faced them as they passed the front and turned down the drive.

'It looks like the place I filmed that costume drama,' said Hayat, as the tyres crunched on gravel. 'I hope there's going to be a handsome stable lad.'

'To make eyes at you over the milk churns?' asked Polly.

'To have an illicit romp with behind a haystack, more like,' said Max.

'The website says it used to be an inn,' Polly said, as they drove beneath a stone archway into what must once have been the inn yard.

'Wow, you guys! This place looks nice!' said Hayat. They retrieved the key from under the doormat and went inside. The door opened into a big tiled hallway. They explored the well-equipped kitchen, smart dining room, and cosy sitting room, which had what looked like the inn's original brass-topped bar at one end. Max immediately ran behind it to play bartender. Hayat joined him and they did an impromptu performance of as much of 'The Master of the House' from *Les Misérables* as they could remember. Which turned out, fortunately for Polly, to be not very much, because while Hayat's acting might have won her huge parts on stage and screen, her singing was terrible.

'Shame we decided against karaoke,' Max said.

There were three bedrooms upstairs, all light and airy with billowy curtains and thick duvets. Then up again, the top floor had a master suite with a four-poster bed, enormous bath, and panoramic views of sheep-spotted fields.

Hayat threw her handbag on the polished dressing table like a Victorian explorer claiming land with a flag, then sprawled onto the enormous bed. The others joined her, messing up its serene white cover.

'I could get used to this,' said Max.

'When I buy my Chelsea penthouse and my Loire château and my Mombasa beach house, I'll have a bed like this,' said Hayat.

'With fifty mattresses, a hundred featherbeds, and a pea underneath?' asked Polly.

'Of course.'

They went back out to the car park, where a smaller building sat across from the house, reflecting it in miniature. It had clearly once been the stable block: there were five arched doors and a large clock set into the apex above. Polly unlocked the middle door, and she and Max swung it open with a flourish.

'Oh my God: a hot tub!' Hayat jumped up and down in excitement.

'Surprise!'

'Didn't bring my bikini though, so I guess we're skinny-dipping,' said Hayat.

'In your dreams,' said Max, as Polly handed Hayat a carrier bag containing her swimsuit.

'What the hell?'

'I literally walked past you into your bedroom, went through your drawers and you didn't notice,' said Polly.

'When?

'This morning, when you were looking for the car keys.'

'Huh.'

'Good thing Polly's not one of your stalker fans,' said Max. He then proceeded to tear off his clothes, revealing the swimming trunks he was wearing underneath. 'Ta-da!'

'Have you been wearing them for the whole journey, just for that dramatic reveal?' asked Polly.

'Yep!' he said proudly.

'Right, let's start the weekend properly!' said Hayat, producing a bottle of expensive-looking champagne.

'Ooh, Pol Roger,' said Max. 'That was Churchill's favourite champagne.' Max was the group's food and drink snob.

'I was given a case as a present,' said Hayat, dismissively. 'Oh, and I brought some of this for you, Poll.' Hayat handed her a bottle of non-alcoholic sparkling wine. 'Probably tastes like piss but there you go.'

They unpacked the car, got changed, and found glasses. Max produced a box of homemade chilli cheese straws.

'I definitely need one of these in each of my four houses, too,' Hayat said, climbing into the jacuzzi with her glass of champagne.

'I thought it was three?' asked Polly, walking round the edge of the tub to find the thermometer.

'Yeah, I added one. I need a Swiss chalet, so I can learn to ski and eat cheese.'

Ten minutes later, flushed and merry from two kinds of bubbles, they heard tyres crunch on the gravel.

'We're not expecting anyone this early, are we? It's only half four,' said Max.

'Oh crap! It's the food!' Polly levered herself out of the jacuzzi, aided by the others, and grabbed a towel. 'Oi, I'm not going out there on my own! Hayat?'

'Poor Tesco. They'll crash the van if the first thing they see is Hayat in a bikini,' said Max.

'That's true,' said Hayat, pouring herself more champagne.

'Well, you'd better come instead then, hadn't you?' Polly said to Max, wrapping herself in a white fluffy dressing gown. He groaned.

'OK, fine, I'll go on my own,' Polly said, slipping flip-flops on and heading for the door, 'But let's just hope they haven't run out of the icing sugar you wanted and decided to substitute it for...' She paused for effect and turned back towards the others, 'demerara!'

Hayat snorted with laughter and added, 'Or worse, swapped your organic stoneground spelt flour for... Everyday Value!'

'Oh, the horror!' Polly moaned.

'OK, OK, I'm going,' Max said, getting out of the tub.

'And make sure they haven't substituted the halal stuff,' Hayat shouted after them, 'I'm not eating fucking veg again all weekend!'

'Yeah, we weren't going to risk that again,' Max reassured her. 'Nadim's buying the meat.'

They dripped out to the car park, where a man in an orange tabard was knocking on the door. They unpacked the crates of groceries, and Max decided to start baking. Polly left him merrily singing along to his party playlist and throwing (organic) digestive biscuits into a blender.

'You'll catch your death doing all that in a wet towel,' Polly said, and he shooed her out of the door whilst singing the wrong words along to *Mr Brightside*.

She returned to the hot tub room. Hayat thrust her glass at Polly, who replenished it and then refilled her own with the non-alcoholic fizz. She looked forward to treating herself to a glass of real champagne later – this stuff really was not that nice. She checked the jacuzzi temperature again.

'Turn it up, will you?' yawned Hayat.

'Not if you want my company,' said Polly, climbing in with Hayat's assistance.

'Oh yeah. Bet you can't wait for that baby to come out. Get back to drinking properly and not having to worry about pâté or hot yoga.'

'Just touching my toes would be nice,' said Polly, lightly.

Hayat had become increasingly detached as Polly's pregnancy had progressed. She clearly resented the alien presence in her best friend's abdomen that was depriving her of said friend's company through nights out and bottles of wine. But however self-centred Hayat could be, and Polly had long ago learned to embrace that as part of who she was, she would never forget how caring she was in a crisis. Hayat had been filming at the time of Polly's miscarriage, and Polly hadn't wanted to disturb her. But Nadim had told her, and she had called in sick and driven through the night to get to Polly. She had listened, hugged, even phoned Polly's mum to get her recipe for rice *congee*. She had stayed with Polly for a fortnight, phoning her increasingly impatient agent with a series of worsening symptoms that she read off the NHS website, in a voice that sounded ever closer to death's door.

'What if they fire you?' Polly had worried, curled up with Hayat on the sofa as they worked their way through *Elementary* and bowls of Hayat's chilli popcorn.

'Too late now – they've nearly finished filming. They'd have to redo it all.'

And yet they had fired her, and her agent had been furious.

'He'll get over it,' Hayat shrugged, but in unguarded moments Polly saw how anxious she was. So Polly went to stay with her parents in Manchester instead, while Hayat picked up the pieces of her career. Which she did, in her usual indomitable form, by landing the lead in a West End show, winning an Olivier award, and being snowed under by offers, including one from the director who had fired her.

'So, what's next after this BBC thing?' Polly asked Hayat, stretching out and enjoying the weightlessness of the water.

Hayat turned to retrieve the champagne bottle. 'Well, we're filming again in January, then I've got that play at the National, and then we'll see,' she said. 'But enough about me. When does your maternity leave start?'

Polly frowned. She had never heard Hayat say 'enough about me' before, and she had certainly never heard her turn the subject away from her career. Hayat had closed her eyes now, leaning her head back on the rim of the hot tub. Was she avoiding eye contact, as well as changing the subject?

Polly was brought back to reality – if sitting in a ferry full of dead people could really qualify as such – by laughter from the three boys opposite her. Two young girls were sitting next to them: one cheery and casual, her blue-streaked braids and school uniform immaculate, the other a terrified mess. She had huge scared eyes in a battered face that had collapsed in on one side, and blood-matted blonde hair that had been tugged out in chunks. The blood had splashed all over her faded yellow pyjamas.

'Right, first things first,' said the girl with braids, 'Let's get you cleaned up a bit and you'll feel better. You don't need to look all dead like that – you can change it by remembering. I'll show you. Look at my hair: you see the braids, right?' The blonde girl nodded. 'So now I'm remembering when I had an afro. Thinking about, like, how I looked, how it felt.' She closed her eyes and moved her head slightly, concentrating. The blue braids recoiled slowly into her scalp, replaced by a buoyant halo of black hair. The blonde girl's eyes grew even bigger.

'But how...?'

'It's just, like, remembering. But instead of the memory being in your head, you make it real. You try. Do your hair, like I done. Think about the last time you made it all nice.' The other girl just looked at her. 'Go on. Close your eyes and imagine that memory.'

The blonde girl obediently scrunched her eyelids closed, sticking out her tongue slightly. Slowly, Polly saw bright curls sprouting from the bare patches of scalp, growing until they reached her shoulders. The blood was replaced by two blue clips pulling her hair into neat symmetry behind her ears. She opened her eyes.

'That's it! You done it! Have a look.' The girl with the afro produced a small blue mirror with a snowman on the back. The blonde girl looked, and finally smiled.

'Can I do my face too?'

'Course!'

Closing her eyes again, the girl's caved-in cheek expanded to match her other one, chubby and dimpled, and a rosy blush extinguished the waxy pallor of exsanguination. She looked in the mirror and beamed. Then she took a closer look at the mirror itself. 'Oh my God! Olaf!' She turned to show the other girl her hairclips. 'Look: Elsa!' And just like that, they began discussing *Frozen*, their traumatic deaths forgotten.

The grumpy South African glared and muttered, 'Bloody racket' as they started a spontaneous duet of *Love is an Open Door.* He drew a brochure from his pocket and disappeared behind it, tutting ostentatiously.

Polly pulled out her own brochure. It looked like a university prospectus from the 1970s. The cover showed a group of smiling people sporting a mixture of deadly wounds and corduroy outfits, under the heading 'Welcome to the Afterlife!'

Inside, an introduction read:

'Hi there! The Afterlife Union Committee wishes you a very warm welcome. We hope you had a pleasant life and assure you that your experience hereafter will be equally fulfilling. We have a range of lively and interesting post-decease options for you to choose from, as detailed in this brochure.

'You will be assigned temporary accommodation in Limbo while your application is processed, during which time you are welcome to come along to Open Days if you are unsure of which afterlife suits your needs. You may also choose to remain longer in Limbo if you have any unfinished business that needs resolving (see p. 218).

'We look forward to welcoming you into one of our illustrious eternities!'

The rest of the brochure was a hefty tome, describing afterlives from Aaru ('boundless reed fields, fertile farming areas, and plentiful hunting grounds, warmed by the Egyptian sun!') to Yomi ('if you can make your way past the boulder you are in for a gloomy and peaceful treat!'). Polly flicked through, noting that the entry requirements did not always fit with the cheery welcome of the first page, specifying only 'those who have completed pilgrimages to the shrines of all current and future saints', or 'applicants who are guilty of theft, witchcraft and/or slander.' There were a surprising number of places aimed at people who had died in combat, and even one for 'those who wasted their lives for unrequited love.' Polly turned to page 218.

'Hidden your will up the chimney and want to make sure it gets found? Killed horribly and eager to see the perpetrator banged up? Or simply want to watch your grandchildren grow up from afar? Then Limbo is the place for you! While many afterlives permit return excursions to the living world on specific dates, Limbo residents can enjoy the freedom of more regular access, for research purposes.'

Polly breathed a sigh of relief, an instinctive action that she only realised afterwards was no longer strictly necessary. She couldn't even contemplate most of the afterlives in the brochure – however nice places like Orun-Rere or The Summerland sounded, she wasn't ready to leave everything she knew behind. Limbo was the place for her, at least until she found out how her baby was.

'We are now approaching the end of our journey,' said the captain. 'We hope to see some of you again and wish the rest of you a pleasant onward journey and eternity.'

They drew up at a dock beneath a long grey building bearing a sign that said, 'Welcome to Limbo.'

Natalie Marlow lives in Nuneaton, Warwickshire, with her family. She was once an obsessive reader and is now an obsessive writer. *Needless Alley* is her first novel.

nemarlowwriter@gmail.com

Needless Alley

CHAPTER ONE

August 1933 – The Birmingham Municipal Bank, Edmund Street

A great belly flattened by gravity. The bedspread rucked in the crook of his back. The girl astride – slender as a whip – a helmet of short dark hair. Joan of Arc with a halo of dust motes. Flowers in the room, spring violets, their petals caught mid-fall. It is a very good exposure. This one is different. Dimpled thighs spread wide and wedged against the thick grey pelt of a male chest. Her stockings are at half-mast and her girdle is about her waist. She is still wearing shoes – the heels are a little worn down. Composition is poor – nothing but a tangle of flesh. Here is another. A bottle-blonde with a mouth like a china doll. Jean Harlow in silk – nipples hard and glossy, precious like garnets. She rests her cheek against a hefty thigh, as her lips disengage from a half-flaccid cock. Framed by soft light and Georgian windows, this is his best effort.

'All is well, Mr Garrett?' There was a slick of sweat on the bank clerk's upper lip. Although sheathed in marble and stone, the vault was airless rather than cool, and the young man, stiff with navy serge, carried the summer discomfort about him like a headache.

'All is as it should be, Mr Jarvis.' William tucked the photographs back in their envelope and placed them in the safety deposit box. He and the bank clerk then locked up. A delicate dance of a process. William put his set of keys in his breast pocket and followed Mr Jarvis to the baize-lined door. The clerk, all manners, allowed William through the doorway first and then bolted up behind him. At which point, Mr Jarvis disappeared: melting into the body of the bank, anonymous in his formal suit, faceless with discretion and order. Trained to be silent, these men. All as it should be.

William stepped out of the bank into the lull of the late workday. Soon the streets would throng with shop girls and office juniors, rushing home to the suburbs and their mothers waiting, tea on the table. But for now, only a few empty trams clattered past, swaying down Union Street, creating clouds of hot dust in their wake. This part of the city was red with Warwickshire clay, the bricks of the buildings warm with it: drapers and bicycle shops, grocers and insurance offices, florists with the last of the summer pinks drooping dismal in buckets: all with old-fashioned frontages a touch soiled with soot. Businesses run for the respectable – sober, quiet, hard-working types, who live and work on the margins of a mouth-watering wealth – the kind who lost their savings in the last crash.

On Cherry Street, he passed a brewer's dray, whose driver tipped his cap towards the Wesleyan Chapel. The road then bent and widened and changed its name, and although William could still hear the rattle of the cart and the heavy pounding of hooves on cobblestones, he was now in a place of quiet order; of three-storey buildings; of Morris Oxfords; of sharp railings shining thick with black paint; nameplates and door furniture polished proud Black Country brass. And then he turned again and was home. Buried between the lawyers of Temple Row and the merchants of New Street, and always in shadow, for the street was so narrow and the buildings so tall, Needless Alley caught little passing trade. But William had glimpsed it. Glimpsed the flashes of Portland stone to the north, the green of the cathedral close, the male figures sometimes gowned, the moneyed and privileged in pinstripe suits. To the south the tills of the shops rang out brash with cash, and powdered women in their furs bought more fur and diamonds, for modest amounts, from the city's wholesalers.

William stopped just before his office and used the window of the *Maison Margot* as a mirror to straighten his tie. He peered through the dirt at the women. A full-figured girl was leaning forward and grinding her fists into the base of her spine, her body curved as she eased her back. Another flicked through a *Film Weekly*; Robert Taylor was on the cover – pouting and kohl-eyed like an ingénue. The woman with the bad back turned around, saw William and gave him a neighbourly smile. He nodded to her but was now more interested in the Rolls-Royce reflected in the glass, parked a short way along the street, half on the pavement, skew-whiff and odd-looking like a liner in dock. It must belong to a client. William doubted the owner was after an unfashionable hat.

He unlocked the door to the building and climbed the narrow stairs up to his office. It was army tidy but a little damp, despite being in the eves. The rent on the place was low and the landlord incurious, so William put up with the mustiness, and the rotten windows, and the peeling linoleum chosen for cheapness when King Edward still reigned. There was an anteroom too, which William used for developing his photographs and making tea. This he did now, brewing it strong and sweetening it with a slug of condensed milk. William was searching for the biscuit tin when he heard the man – tread weighty, breathing laboured – tap on the glass of the open door and enter.

He was a heavy man in his late forties, sweating from the short climb up the stairs and heat of the day and patting his face with a large white handkerchief. William had not yet sat down but motioned to his client to take a seat opposite his desk. The fat man did so with relief.

'Mr William Garrett?'

'I am he.' *Let us be formal*, thought William.

'I understand that your discretion is guaranteed, Mr Garrett.'

'I'm not one of life's great talkers.' William settled in his chair, lit a cigarette and drank tea – waited.

'I have an unusual problem.' The fat client was still patting his great, sweaty face – perhaps more out of nerves than heat. 'My wife and I have become estranged. She is somewhat younger than I and—'

'You're not from Birmingham?' *A self-made man but not made here.*

'No, Coventry. My name is Moreton. I'm in hosiery. Ladies' stockings and undergarments.'

'Don't worry about that Mr Moreton, I've seen it all.' There was a pause.

'No, you misunderstand me. That is my business.' Mr Moreton smiled and finally put away his hankie. 'Oh, I see. Yes, a joke. It has been done before, Mr Garrett. I didn't pick up on it because of my nerves. I've been nervy of late.' He offered William his card.

William glanced at it. Feminine curlicues and a stockinged leg. Very fashionable. 'What do you want from me, Mr Moreton?' He watched as Moreton took a breath, like a boy preparing to give a speech.

'Have you ever been in love, Mr Garrett?' *This one loves not wisely but too well.*

'I once put a deposit down on a dining suite for a girl from Tamworth.'

'What happened?'

'I lost ten bob.'

'Well, I imagine it's best not to be a romantic in your line of work. I'm a romantic. It's my chief failing. It rather explains my current predicament.'

'Please, go on.' *I predict your predicament. Your wife is fucking someone else.*

'You see, my young wife and I are ill-suited. I have a new friend, a more mature lady. An excellent woman. My wife has taken a flat in Birmingham. I hardly see her. She now runs with a very fast crowd – bohemians, artists, poets.' He paused and waved his hand in the air in a strangely theatrical manner, as if he needed to show a physical dismissal of bohemians in general. 'I encouraged the painting at first, lessons and so on, because of my fondness for her – a weakness, really. But now I feel she is taking advantage. My new friend refuses to be named in a divorce petition. Absolutely refuses. And besides, our friendship is all above board. I am an honourable man.'

William sighed and rubbed his temples with his thumb and forefinger. He was getting a headache. 'The easiest thing for you, is to come to some kind of agreement with your wife.'

'No, no. It won't work. I tell you, she is happy as she is. I fund it all.

The flat, her little car – which was given to her so that she could come home to me with ease – well, she sold it! Sold it! She runs up bills, and I just pay out. She has no money of her own. She modelled the hosiery. Her legs, Mr Garrett, are exceptional.' Moreton paused and simpered. 'That's what she did before we married. She was the mannequin for my business.'

'Even so, your wife may prefer a financial settlement instead of a nasty divorce. Divorce and a fat allowance could be an incentive for her.' William took a long, final drag of his fag and then stubbed it out. 'Offer her freedom, Mr Moreton, and a good chunk of your money. You'll be amazed at how amenable she'll be.'

'I refuse to support two women.' The words dripped with faux outrage and they irritated William. 'I mean that my new lady would dislike it. Would see it as a betrayal. Clara, my wife, is like an indulgence. An expensive indulgence.' The fat man glanced at his manicured nails. 'It was an unfortunate marriage. I shall admit it.'

'You believe she has a lover? I'll need details.'

Mr Moreton inched forward, and his chair creaked a little under his weight. 'No, that's my problem. I don't believe she has a lover. I had another man follow her; he called himself a detective; he was from Leamington Spa of all places. That's why I've come to you – Birmingham. You were highly recommended by a solicitor friend – a Mr Shirley – you know him?' *Shifty Shirley. The man who looks like a cat. Pretty company you keep.*

'We nod to each other occasionally. I'm sure Mr Shirley has informed you that you can only divorce your wife if she commits adultery. And, you must have substantive proof of any adulterous act. That's the law of the land.' William's tone was cold. It was a game he had to play with all his clients. *But she has a lover. I'd put a fiver on it. Let me sniff him out. Leamington Spa knows fuck all.*

Moreton's eyes narrowed a little. Again, he waved those pudgy, fidgety hands of his, as though he was trying to catch the correct words; finally he said, 'She has a potentiality.'

'I've never heard it called that before.'

Mr Moreton gave an exasperated sigh. 'She may not have a lover, but she has a potentiality – or a susceptibility, perhaps.' He glanced over to the camera sitting on top of William's filing cabinet, avoiding eye contact. 'Clara is susceptible to handsome men. I feel sure of it.'

William offered Mr Moreton a wry smile and said, 'Don't worry, Mr Moreton. I know what you mean. We just have to find the right man and the right circumstances and then you will have your divorce.'

'Yes, yes, find the right man. They said you would understand.'

'I'm a very understanding man, Mr Moreton. I'm also very expensive.'

The fat man grinned. Finally, he seemed comfortable. 'Men who are motivated by money, Mr Garrett, are the only men I trust.'

'Excellent. I will need one hundred pounds as a retainer. I recommend that you pay me in cash. It could take some time to arrange things. Once firm evidence is in place, you will review it, and if you consider it satisfactory then you pay me a further two hundred. I may need to contact you for extras – maids, waiters and so forth will need incentives. However, I always attempt to avoid that scenario. Our arrangements are best kept discreet.' William lit another cigarette, but this time offered one to Moreton. 'Do you have a good photograph of her? Something recent?' Moreton nodded. 'I'll need her address, obviously. Names of friends, acquaintances.' William sat back in his chair and relaxed a little. 'Of course, if I find she has a lover, which is likely, the price is half. I'm not a thief.'

Mr Moreton, who had refused William's cigarette, now proceeded to take a bag of boiled sweets from his jacket pocket. He offered one to William: 'Humbug, Mr Garrett?'

CHAPTER TWO
The Black Horse, Bristol Street

It was a Friday when William sat next to Clara Moreton on the tram. Her summer frock was flimsy floral and stuck to her skin with the sweat of the day. He could smell linseed oil and oranges, for she had a basket of fruit which she gripped tight – her fingers mucky with paint, hands like a boy, nails stubby and bitten, the flesh creamy and soft. William closed his eyes for a time and allowed the sway of the tram to press his knee into her thigh. Clara Moreton was not wearing stockings or even a slip. William had seen the outline of her body as the sun shone through her dress that morning – the curve of her belly and hips in shadow, the ripe pear of an arse flaring out from her waist. It was the fag end of rush hour, and the tram was still full, so he chanced this closeness.

And, such closeness was the nearest Clara Moreton had been to a man all week. William fidgeted in his seat and moved a fraction nearer; felt the heat of her against his leg. *Here I am – now, you feel me.* Seven days of shadowing had resulted in nothing. She was a worker, no doubt – daubing at her canvases all day in that flat of hers in Hockley – and, whatever Moreton claimed, his wife lived simply: a visit to the haberdashery at Lewis's for mending thread; tea and something on toast at a café; a basket of fruit from the Bull Ring at the end of the day. And, no lover. No oily fancy man with orchids and chocolates in hand. No room booked under the name of Smith at some nice little roadhouse just outside of Warwick.

She left the tram halfway down Bristol Street, and William let her.

Not following but watching through the window as she walked towards the doors of that sprawling, modern pub – the gables of ye olde England, Formica bar, bold horse brasses made last week in Wolverhampton. Shit beer. He got off at the next stop with a crowd of housewives who were weighed down with bags of fancy goods – *tinned fruit is just as nice as the real thing – no, sweeter, better.* The women stopped abruptly as the tram sailed onward. They were looking at the sky. The clouds high and heavy, grey and fat like zeppelins. Below the clouds, a vapour trail. The aeroplane a buzzing fly. William stood for a second and watched. The machine was spelling something out, looping and returning. A 'b' perhaps, and an 'i' and then a 'r': an advertisement.

'It's for custard!' A woman was shouting and pointing. 'Yes, yes! Look! *BIRDS*!'

'He should spell out *CUSTARD*. You can't just write *BIRDS* in the sky. It's too odd. Confusing.'

The women waited for the rest of the message, frowning. But the aeroplane had gone for good, and the small party soon scattered outward into the streets of new villas which branched off Bristol Street. William crossed the road, making for The Black Horse and Clara Moreton.

She was there, at the main bar, standing with a rangy man in baggy tweeds. The place was empty, save for another young couple, scrubbed and respectable, sipping beer and holding hands. William ordered a pint of mild and stood away from Clara. He pulled an American novel out of his jacket pocket and began to read. It was about a man who bought whisky from gangsters. Then one of them raped a girl with a corncob.

'What are the oranges for?' The thin man asked.

'I'll paint them later. They sell their fruit cheap at the end of the day. I came straight from the Bull Ring.'

'Shall I give you a lift back?'

'My God! This place is cavernous!' Clara looked around. Her eyes flickered at William for a scant moment. He looked down and continued to read. 'Why here?'

'It's pleasant for the ladies.'

'Are you serious?'

'A schooner of sherry for the little woman, barkeep.' The rangy man winked.

'Please don't be clever with the staff. Anyway, I prefer beer. Or gin.'

'G and Ts all round.'

'When are the others arriving?'

He looked at his watch. 'I did say half past.'

At which point a crowd billowed in through the double doors, seven or eight of them, their laughter shrill and dominating. The courting couple jumped.

'Well, this is all very pleasant.' A youngster, fair-haired and tall, wearing working man's boots and expensive trousers.

'I'll have a filled roll.' It was a woman, mannish in slacks – unlike the men, she was wearing a tie. Not the sherry-sipping type.

Another man joined them. He was a head shorter than William, running to fat and trying, but failing, to disguise his paunch with a Fair Isle sweater. His fashionable moustache was a trimmed strip above his lips, and his eyes were rimmed red. *A drinker or a crier.* The mannish woman offered a brief nod and a weak smile, but the rest of the group did not greet him. *The outcast – the hanger-on.*

'Why are we here?' Another woman, small and no more than a girl, struggling to mask her broad Birmingham vowels.

'That's what Clara asked,' said the thin man.

'I think they call it brewer's Tudor.' The young man in the heavy boots seemed pleased, he was looking about the empty room. 'I like it very much. It's quite, quite Warwickshire.'

'There are more women now. It's pleasant for them. The city pubs are so dive-y.'

'It's the sort of place one brings one's mistress.' Another man – the kind who could afford to keep a woman.

'If one is a bank manager.'

'Clara, were you ever a mistress?'

'Reader, I married him.' Clara smiled at the man. Rich and in his twenties, he was a matinee idol of a boy, with swathes of dark hair worn without brilliantine and a little long at the back. William wore his hair like his father – freshly cut and slathered in Macassar oil.

'My dear, you have never been obscure, plain and little.' *God, he kissed her hand.*

'We should really get started.' It was the rangy man again.

The group drifted towards a cluster of tables which the men pulled together, scraping the legs across the linoleum and leaving the scuff marks for the landlady to sort in the morning. William saw the barman frown. The young couple got up from their seats and headed for the ladies' lounge. He could no longer hear the group clearly, but there were snippets of clarity, and laughter – plenty of laughter.

'There is power in a collective.' The blonde in hobnail boots.

'Well, you would say that.'

'I'm rather tired of craft. We are always associated with craft. It's even in the bloody coat of arms.' *Watch it love, your accent's showing.*

'I really don't think that's the point.'

'The surrealists work with photographs. Their collage work is remarkable.'

'Yes, remarkable.'

'Are they obscene?'

'Breton?'

'No, no. My photographs – would you say they were obscene?' The outsider.

'Must we have this conversation again?'

'In all honesty, I don't like the razor blades.'

'It is an anti-fascist tool. We can fight them with it. They do not understand it.' It was the beautiful prince charming who could kiss a lady's hand and not look a fool. William felt a flutter of jealousy.

'We can talk politics later.'

'There are Spanish artists who—'

'Think about Buñuel and his films. They say they are obscene – but nothing is as obscene as fascism.'

'No, no. Not Spain again. We must concentrate.'

'I'm not talking of Spain. You think of Spain when I talk of fascism. And, you think of Chancellor Hitler and his *Ermächtigungsgesetz*. It is Birmingham, I talk of. They're here, here now – Mosley and his thugs. We must use our art, our poetry – even journalism – to counter these monsters.' Beautiful and earnest, the dark-haired boy made a lovely speech.

'Why must you dominate every meeting with your own particular brand of rather naïve dogma? This is a collective of artists – *artists*. You Trots have your own get-togethers, I'm sure.' It was the outsider who spoke, waspish – like an old maid.

'Good God, man. Do you not know the true purpose of art? Art is freedom.'

'Oh, dear me. How young you are.'

Then, quietness. One or two of the group shifted in their seats. The men stared into their beer. It was the mannish woman who broke the silence – the diplomat of the group. 'Eileen talks well on Freud. She practically revels in penis envy. Freud has so much to offer us, I feel. The workings of the mind transcend mere politics. Eileen agrees. She feels that psychoanalysis will help us explore more than simply superficial realities. This surely is what we have in common – the psyche.' *Realpolitik, well done love.*

'Foolish.' Clara, now.

'Freud or Eileen?'

'Both.' Clara smiled.

'Why are you here, Clara? Everything you do is so very – realistic – all of those stained kitchen sinks.' The mannish woman lit a cigar. *A cigar!*

'And naked charwomen. She's very good with a "lady who does".' It was the rangy man.

'Oh, my goodness, yes. Clara darling, I do adore your chars. Your realism is duly forgiven.'

'Does it matter what kind of art we make? What matters is that we assert ourselves.' The blonde in heavy boots. *Another public school Marxist.*

'The purest surrealist act is walking into a crowd with a loaded gun.' *Shush, Clara. What do you know of loaded guns?*

'Clara is the true anarchist of the group.'

'And she quotes Breton.'

They all laughed.

The group went on like this for some time – their talk feverish, their listening listless. They bored William, but Clara looked on bright-eyed, devoted, her conversation fervent. Happy. Happy talking, clutching her basket of oranges. William drank another pint. All hell was breaking loose in the book he was reading. The raped girl was being kept as the gangster's mistress now – in a brothel. There may have been a moral to the story but, try as William might, he just couldn't fathom it.

It was a little after midnight before Clara showed up at Vyse Street. William was surprised to see her arrive with the rangy man. The man drove hugging the kerb, slowly cautious in drink, until he was thirty feet away or so from Clara's flat, then leapt out of the motor with gawky energy to open the passenger door for the lady. Clara Moreton tumbled out, holding tight to her basket of oranges, but then teetered on the pavement as though peering over a great cliff edge. William was hunched in the doorway of the Rose Villa Tavern but could see Clara quite clearly. Under the gas lamp, she seemed prettily vulnerable – pissed-up and pouting, her dress still clinging, and her hair now ruffled. The thin man held her by the waist as if she were about to fall. Clara smiled up at the man. William thought that they might kiss, but kisses mean nothing. They stood in the light for just a moment further, and then stumbled towards Clara's front door. Her arm was raised about the thin man's shoulder; her hip was tilted drunkenly into his. William was reminded of a sentimental postcard he had seen towards the end of the war – *Tender Comrades.* When she had disentangled herself from him, and unlocked the door to her flat, the thin man slapped her on the arse, hard. He blew her kisses and called her darling – acting the clown because he lacked the looks for a proper seduction. She shook her head; he whispered something in her ear; she shook her head again. *Not that drunk, then.* The thin man had been rebuffed, so turned towards his car and laughed and waved as he went – walking backwards, comedy bowing and scraping, still blowing his kisses. Clara laughed. *An admirable retreat. He'll live to fight another day.*

William thought about the American novel. In it, the gangster couldn't fuck the girl. He couldn't get it up. One of his lads had to do it for him whilst he watched, secretly. But he wasn't content with looking, the gangster – it was just his lot, to be the voyeur, to be the cuckold. William reckoned that he understood the book now. Morality was immaterial. There was only human behaviour, most of which was bad. And sometimes, very rarely, people caught the consequences of their actions and were forced to pay their dues.

Nicola Monaghan has published four novels and several novellas. She won a Betty Trask Award, the Authors' Club Best First Novel Award and the Waverton Good Read for her first novel, *The Killing Jar*. Her short, gritty films have starred household names such as Brendan Coyle and Steven Arnold.

niki.valentine@gmail.com
www.nicolamonaghan.com

Dead Flowers

1967

A WHITER SHADE OF PALE

It was Saturday night glad times in the Loggerheads pub and Harry was propping up the bar with his pal Bobby O'Quaid. An old man a couple of tables away tipped a hat at the pair of them.

The three old crows who sat together in the corner most nights and drank gin until they fell over were cackling away. The eldest one shouted out. 'Oi, Harry, come and chat with us, duck.'

Bobby turned to him with one raised eyebrow. 'They're after your body again, Harry. Watch 'em, that's all I'm saying.'

'Well, I've never had sisters before, so I might be tempted,' Harry said, laughing and slapping Bobby on the back. He stood up and headed towards their table.

The three women grinned at Harry as he approached. Not one of them had a full head of hair and their mouths were missing several teeth, except the smallest who had giveaway perfect chops that could only be false. 'Hello, my lovelies,' he said. 'What are you lassies up to tonight?'

'Gladys's brought her tarots,' one of them said. The one with the false gnashers was holding a pack of cards.

'I'll do a reading for you, if you want, me duck,' Gladys told him. 'You don't have to cross me palm with silver or owt like that. I just like the cut of your jib.'

'Oh, I dunno,' Harry said. 'I dinnae think you ought to mess with that sort of thing.' His voice was playful, though, at odds with the words. 'Ah, gwaan then. What harm's in it?'

Gladys glanced up at him through her lashes, looking weirdly coquettish. She handed him the deck to shuffle. Then she took the cards back and started dealing them on to the table in a cross formation. Harry had seen this before; his Granny Mac used to do the tarot. She swore by them and would deal the cards whenever she had a decision to make.

The old woman turned the cards face up, one then another, announcing them as she went. Bobby strolled across and watched over Harry's shoulder.

'The King of Swords,' Gladys said, 'oh my goodness.' She turned more cards. 'Now don't be startled, young man. This un's death but don't take it all literal.'

Harry stared at the card and play-acted a dramatic shiver, making the old ladies laugh. Gladys continued to turn cards over slowly and announce their names. 'The Three of Swords.' Turn. 'The Wheel of Fortune.' Turn. 'The Lovers.' This card had a picture of a half-naked couple on it, wrapped up in each other and tangled with ivy.

'Ooh err, naughty,' said Bobby at that one, elbowing Harry with a smirk on his face.

'There's a bright future for you here,' Gladys said, looking at Harry with a level gaze. She glanced down at the table with a frown. 'Your heart's desire. This pub, or some lady, or summat else you have your heart set on, that'll come to you.'

Harry let out a comic gasp, then clasped his hand over his mouth.

'More than that,' she said. 'The whole shebang. You'll be king of your world, whatever that means.' Gladys smiled in a far-off way.

The tallest woman spoke, her voice rich and deep. 'King of the Hoop,' she said, her words like an echo. She pointed at a card. 'Wheel of Fortune,' she said, 'and the King of Swords.' She smiled and tapped the side of her nose, as if there was an in-joke that Harry should know about.

Gladys turned her head to take in the whole cross again.

Bobby pointed at the Lovers card. 'What's this 'un about?' he said, winking at Harry.

'The Lovers points to good marriage, and happiness,' the third old bird piped up.

'What about me?' Bobby nudged Harry again. He looked like he was enjoying this a bit too much.

'You'll do all right,' Gladys said. 'You'll be happy, in the end.'

'Dunno about that. Fame and fortune sounds better, if I'm being honest.'

Gladys smiled like she knew all the secrets in the world. She stared down at the cross she'd made. 'I see something good here for your children,' she said, and left it at that.

'What about my weans?' Harry said. 'How many? Will they be happy and rich?' He was grinning and catching Bobby's high mood.

Gladys grabbed the cards and cleared them quickly. 'The Tarot don't tell you everything,' she said.

The women turned towards each other then, and back to their glasses of gin and orange. Whatever they had wanted from Harry, it was over now.

'What the hell was that about?' Bobby said, as they walked back to the bar.

Harry shrugged. He wasn't smiling anymore. The way she'd suddenly packed up the cards when he'd asked that question about children had put the willies up him.

They stood at the bar and he ordered two more pints of mild. He thought about the cards. The Wheel of Fortune and the King of Swords, whatever that meant. The pints were handed over and he took a big gulp. Bobby stood beside him, staring into space as he took his first sup.

'Penny for 'em,' Bobby said.

'I dinnae know,' Harry said. He took another gulp of his drink and shrugged. 'I dinnae believe in that shite, anyways,' he said. But he closed his eyes and all he could see was a picture from the cards; three swords piercing a heart, and blood. Blood, gurgling and bubbling and thickening like it was boiling in a pot, leaking all over the floor of the pub and pooling at his feet.

2011
HOME

Sian dropped the box on the bedroom floor and a cloud of dust flew up, making her cough. Kris appeared at the door carrying two boxes with such ease that he made them look empty.

'I see we have the usual Sian Love approach going on here,' he said. He walked over and placed his boxes carefully against the wall. 'You'll break your stuff.'

'I barely own anything breakable,' she said.

Kris turned towards her and raised one eyebrow. 'Previous house moves?'

'Oi!' Sian aimed a playful slap at his shoulder and he ducked away from her. She headed towards the stairs. She heard his footsteps following her back down and turned. She couldn't help smiling as she caught his eyes.

'How you manage to run a methodical lab and not just break all the test tubes is beyond me.' His voice was teasing, but Sian could tell this was something he'd thought about before.

'Work's different,' she said, taking his teasing seriously. 'I have to make sure samples don't get mixed up and I don't end up framing someone innocent. I'm handling people's DNA, all their innermost secrets. It's more important than stuff.'

Kris grinned. 'It suits me if you break things. Gives you an excuse to call someone tall, dark and handsome to help you fix it all up,' he said.

'Excuse me, but I can fix my own things, thanks.'

'I'm just trying to help you here, giving you some good excuses for getting me over. Your loss if you can't see that this is for your benefit.'

Sian swung herself off the stairs and into the hallway, holding onto the post at the bottom of the banister. Something about being back at the Loggerheads pub after all these years made her feel teenaged again. Kris grabbed her and pulled her into a kiss. She let him. It was easier than getting into another discussion about how much time he might end up spending here and how it was such a big place for one person. She pulled away and noticed Elvis sitting neatly and calmly by the back door.

'You need to bark, boy!' she said, opening it wide for him. 'I'm not psychic.'

'Maybe he is,' Kris said.

'Police training's good,' she said. 'But not that good.'

Elvis strolled outside and dug at the same patch of concrete again. Sian watched him, concerned. 'I wish he'd stop doing that,' she said, shivering.

'Ah, he just wants to dig, man. You need to get that concrete up and give your good boy a proper garden so he can enjoy his retirement.'

Sian nodded. She'd planned to do that anyway and was a bit annoyed at her boyfriend for thinking he needed to guide her. But he was only trying to help and she was being unreasonable. She wondered if she was broken in some way. She hated the idea that she might be because it meant that he-who-must-not-be-named had achieved what he set out to do to her.

'Tea?' Kris asked her, cutting across her thoughts with a warm smile.

'That'd be nice,' she said. It would be nice. And Kris was nice, wasn't he? She really needed to get over whatever was holding her back with him and prove she wasn't broken. She would try harder.

Sian sat down on one of the fold-out chairs in the kitchen as the kettle boiled. She'd scrubbed and scrubbed the cupboards and surfaces in here but the colours still looked muted by grime. She wasn't sure she would ever get the place clean. Kris got up and dug in the boxes on the worktop, pulling out some teabags and a couple of mugs. He turned towards Sian. 'OK, Dr Love. I've known you for long enough now. What's wrong?'

Sian shook her head. 'Nothing.'

He popped teabags into the mugs, then rolled his eyes. 'Don't give me that. It's never nothing. I'm not that stupid.'

She let out a long sigh. 'Oh, I dunno. Can't put my finger on it. Just being back here.'

Kris glanced across at her and for a horrible moment Sian thought he was about to come over and hug her or something. But perhaps he really had known her long enough. He carried on making the tea and then brought the mugs over, plonking one down in front of her on the pasting table that she was using as her temporary dining furniture.

'It's probably just the circumstances. Y'know. Inheriting the place? Your uncle dying? That stuff's hard, even if you tell yourself it isn't.'

'I don't tell myself anything.'

'That's not what I mean.'

They let the silence rest for a moment and both sipped at tea. Sian cupped her hands around the mug and felt it warm her. 'It's not that,' she said. 'It's this place.'

A loud scratching sound came from the other side of the kitchen door along with a gentle whimper, as if on cue.

'See what I mean?' she said. She got up and walked into the hallway; Kris followed. They both watched Elvis, who was scratching at the cellar door. 'Leave it, boy,' she said. Then, louder. 'Leave it!' Elvis came away, a good boy. 'He keeps doing that,' she said.

'He's just being a dog. He wants to explore.' Kris's eyes glinted. 'Maybe he read online that there's a cave down there.'

'Not this again.'

'Ah, c'mon, Sianey. Don't you wanna see what's down there? It's just behind the cellar, I know it is.' His face lit up with the thought of it and Sian couldn't help smiling at him. 'Yes!' he said, doing a victory thrust with one hand. He rushed off down the hallway and all Sian could think was that she hadn't said yes at all. She'd just smiled, and only a bit.

Kris was back at the door with the toolbox in his hand and a huge grin across his face. He stopped dead, catching Sian's mood.

'Can we go out or something? Get a drink?' She looked down at her feet. 'I could do with a drink.'

'OK,' Kris said. He placed the toolkit down next to the door. 'Why not?'

Sian grabbed her coat from where she'd slung it over the top of the living room door. Elvis padded after her. 'Not this time, boy,' she said. She checked her pocket for her keys. Glancing up, she saw Kris locking the back door. As if he lived here, too.

Kris walked past her and out into the street. Sian turned, taking a last look at Elvis. 'You be a good boy,' she said. 'No digging or scratching at that door. OK?'

He tipped his head to the side, as if trying to understand what she was saying.

She smiled at him, which made him tip his head to the other side.

'You coming?' Kris said, yards up the street already.

Sian turned from her dog and shut the door.

'My uncle used to call this place Twat Church,' Sian said, gesturing around at the drinkers in what used to be the Unitarian Church, before it was bought and renovated by an upmarket pub chain.

Kris laughed loudly and brought a hand to his mouth, as if the beer he'd just swallowed needed holding in. 'You shouldn't swear like that, young lady. In the house of God!'

'Yeah, well, God moved out a while ago, and all the twats moved in.' The old building was packed with drunk, noisy groups; more than one of them looked like stag parties. A few tables away, someone shouted 'who are ya' and his friends joined in so loudly it swallowed all the air.

Sian bent her neck back to look at the high ceiling and the stone arches along the side that had been turned into balconies. There were several large stained-glass windows and even the mirrors on the walls were shaped to fit with this style. It was very in keeping with where the building had come from.

'Better to turn things into pubs than to turn pubs into something else,' Kris said.

Sian gave him a level stare. 'The Loggerheads hasn't made any money for about a million years.'

'Yeah, but maybe your uncle wasn't a businessman. With Dr Sian Love at the helm, it could be a very different story.' He placed a hand on her waist.

'Oh, my uncle was very definitely a businessman.'

'Oh, really?' There was a sudden light in his eyes. 'A "businessman"?' He made air quotes with one hand.

Sian nodded.

'Your family gets more interesting by the second.'

'Believe me, they really don't.' Sian turned from him, wriggling herself from under his grip and heading for a nearby table. They sat down.

'So, what's bugging you about the house then, babe?' Kris said. 'You feeling creeped out by the ghosts?'

'Ghosts?' Sian recoiled. He was sounding a bit like her mum right now. Sian was pretty sure that Kris didn't believe in this kind of thing any more than she did. They'd been on enough crime scenes together when Sian worked for Notts Police to know that the dead didn't hang about; what always struck you was the sense of absence.

'Whoo-oo-ooo!' Kris said, making a token effort of waving a hand and wiggling his fingers. 'Nah, I don't mean that at all. Memories, the past, you know?'

'Oh, so not ghosts at all then.'

'You know what I mean,' he said. And Sian thought that she didn't, really, and that he said this to her a lot.

Sian took a deep breath, as if she was about to dive underwater, then another sip of her beer. 'OK,' she said. She decided she would talk about it, make an effort to open up to him. 'Yes, memories. I ran away to the pub, when I was fifteen. I'd just found out that David wasn't my real dad and I was furious. Uncle Bob took me in but he told my mother I was there and she turned up screaming like a banshee.' She stared down at the table, remembering it so clearly, the twist to her mum's face. She'd thought it was rage at the time, pure, blind anger, but now, as she tried to picture it again, she saw fear there instead. 'She threatened to drag me out of the pub by my hair.' She was shaking her head and, to her horror, she felt the prickle of tears in her eyes. She pulled them back. 'I've never seen her like that before or since,' she said. 'I still don't know what it was about.'

Kris looked thoughtful and was quiet for a moment. 'Quite a big deal, something like that. What it does to a family. I'm not surprised at her reaction,' he said.

A sip of drink, marking time whilst she gave herself space to think. 'It wasn't that. At least, it wasn't just that.'

'How d'you find out? Birth certificate?'

Sian let out a bitter little laugh. 'No, nothing as simple as that. It's David's name on my birth certificate. But he has the wrong colour eyes.'

'You what?'

Sian waved her beer about as if to illustrate what she was saying. 'You can blame good old-fashioned 'O' level biology,' she said. 'Two blue-eyed parents can't have a brown-eyed child, etcetera. I read that, and kept staring in the mirror to see if my eyes were really some kind of odd shade of green that gave the impression of brown, or had some blue in there somewhere, right in the middle near my iris. I tried to persuade myself that what I'd read had to be wrong. But it nagged at me until I blurted something out in the middle of a row like a total cliché. You know the drill, the "you're not my dad!" obligatory teenage strop kind of moment.'

'Did they deny it?' Kris's eyes were shining.

'Well I was bloody expecting them to but no. My mum just crumbled. She sat down, looking like I'd knocked all the air out of her. And she said, no, he's not. And then started giving me the third degree about who had told me. When I explained about the eyes, she seemed relieved.' Sian shook her head. 'I couldn't believe they'd lied to me all those years. Lied to the bloody registrar too, the pair of them. Mind you, poor old Dad. I mean, David dad. He probably didn't know that long before I did. I dunno. He just seemed gobsmacked by the whole thing.'

Kris had gone very quiet and was staring at her. She hadn't meant to say as much as this. She imagined he was going off her by the second.

'Anyway,' she said, running a hand through her dark, cropped hair. 'It was all wrong, my premise. I know that now. There are a bunch of ways that blue-eyed parents can have brown-eyed kids. My genetic father might very well have blue eyes for all I know. It's all much more complicated than that biology class.' She paused and looked at Kris. 'I just happened to have been right at the same time as being wrong,' she said.

'Oh my God, Sianey, that's fucking mental.'

'Yup.'

'And you said your family wasn't that interesting,' he said.

'Fucked up is not the same as interesting.'

They both sipped beer at the same time and their eyes caught. Kris put his glass down and reached across the table for Sian's hand. 'No wonder you don't like the place.'

'It's not that.' She swilled her beer around the bottle like she was looking for something in the liquid. 'I dunno. I don't think so, anyway. It's the way my mum was. I can't explain it.'

'It was probably just the shock of finding out,' he said. 'That would have made everything feel weird.'

'Maybe,' Sian said, but she wasn't convinced. She leaned back in her chair and looked around the crowded bar. She considered getting another drink but decided she couldn't be bothered. 'Listen, I'm knackered. I'm going to go home.'

'And you need a tall, handsome young man to keep an eye on you, protect you from those ghosts?' Even his voice knew he was pushing his luck with that one.

'I just want to get an early night. Sleep off this mood and start fresh tomorrow,' she said.

'You're biting off your nose to spite your face, young lady.'

'You know that neither of us are actually young, don't you?' she said.

Kris downed the last of his beer, then shook his head. 'What's wrong, Sianey? We getting a bit too close?'

'No, I'm just tired.'

Kris stood up and put on his jacket. 'Fine,' he said. 'Your loss.' He waited for a moment, like he was expecting her to change her mind. Then he zipped up his coat and walked away.

Sian watched him go. She felt like everyone in the bar was watching him leave, watching the two of them. But, actually, he was walking slowly, with his usual, lazy swagger and she wouldn't even have known he was pissed off, except he was leaving without so much as a kiss on the cheek. She wished she could stop upsetting him and just be normal. One day, he'd decide he'd had enough of her nonsense. But she couldn't help it.

It wasn't so much that she was broken, she remembered, but more that she was different in some way. *Mad, mental, psycho*, just like her evil ex-boyfriend had said.

'Gary,' she said. 'Gary, Gary, Gary.' As if saying his name aloud enough times might undo the hex he'd put on her life.

Yeah, there it was, exactly what he'd told her so many times. She wasn't like other people at all.

CELLAR

Sian came down the steep steps past the Contemporary Art Gallery, trying to make out the Nottingham lace patterns in its concrete walls, then to the tiny street of mostly ex-council houses that stood in a crescent at the bottom. She could feel the history around her, Narrow Marsh, as it used to be, full of crime and squalor. It was odd how that made her feel at home.

The sign from the old Loggerheads pub was swinging in the wind, making a crashing sound against its frame. She could hear Elvis, barking and howling the other side of the door. He wasn't usually that bothered when she went out for a couple of hours but the combination of the high winds and being somewhere new was probably to blame. She dug into her bag to get her keys and his barking got more urgent. 'It's just me, you silly sod,' she said. She opened the door and he came bounding over, doing the dance of love he did whenever she came home, nuzzling her, then rocking from back-to-front paws. She leaned down to give the German Shepherd a proper scratch behind his ears and let him lick her nose, then locked and bolted the front door, shutting out Narrow Marsh and the dark.

Elvis ran through the hallway to the back door. She grabbed the key from a hook on the wall; he was trying to force the door open before she could unlock it. Finally, he burst outside and jumped into the air, barking at the night sky. It felt chilly with the door open so Sian went into the kitchen and turned the heating on. She wasn't sleepy enough for bed. She rooted through the boxes searching for something to drink, and glasses. She could only find an old bottle of Amaretto and the plastic beakers from the bathroom. Sian poured herself a drink and slipped through to the living room, collapsing on the sofa and kicking off her shoes.

Sitting back, she tried to relax. She took a sip from her drink. It had a thickness and a rich, high taste. She couldn't shake the idea that part of the slick flavour was old toothpaste. She heard Elvis, scratching at the cellar door again. She ignored him for as long as she could. Then he popped his head into the room and stared at her. 'Fine,' she said, putting down her drink and walking back through to the hall. She closed and locked the back door. 'I can see I'm not going to get any peace here. Let's go and have a look.'

Sian opened the cellar door and flicked a switch; the light down there came on for a moment, then the bulb blew. 'How's that for a sign,' she muttered, then laughed at herself. Her toolbox was beside the door, where Kris had left it. She opened it and found a torch. Then she picked up the box in case she needed the tools when she got down there. Elvis scratched at the door again, then looked up at her expectantly. 'You know, boy, the rule is never go down into the cellar.' She smiled at her own joke. And then she pushed open the door and he barged past her and rushed down the stairs, barking.

Sian followed him, shining the torch ahead of her. She tripped slightly as she misjudged the last step, then righted herself. At the bottom of the stairs there was a high, sweet smell, reminiscent of old bins. She put the toolbox down on the floor. Elvis was scratching at the far wall, and turned towards her, barking. He started to whimper, and then pace the floor in a way she'd never seen him do before.

It was as if the temperature of the room had suddenly dropped, the way people say it does when they think they see ghosts. Of course, Sian knew better than that. She knew this was simply another effect of adrenaline on her body. But the feeling struck home, nonetheless. Because Elvis wasn't any old retired police dog. He was a cadaver dog. Elvis had been trained to find the dead.

Niamh O'Connor is a bestselling Irish author of fiction and non-fiction who worked as true crime editor of the *Sunday World* newspaper for over ten years. She has a degree in English literature and previous Master of Arts degrees in journalism and screenwriting. Studying at UEA was a lifelong dream.

crackingcrime@gmail.com

Mapping Keira

Jamie lay in bed staring at the ceiling. He was so clammy he could have peeled the sheets off like an extra layer of skin, but he hadn't moved in several hours. He was too scared he'd do the thing. He'd promised himself last time never again. And the time before that... and the time before that...

2 a.m. *and counting.*

He rolled onto his side and stared at the revision timetable tacked to the wall over the desk, every day since last September crossed out. All that work wasted. Tomorrow he was due to sit his final Leaving Certificate exam papers in physics and chemistry. Then the countdown would begin to the results and finding out if he'd got enough points to study veterinary medicine. It was the job he wanted more than anything else in the world.

He put his hands on his head, which felt like a pressure cooker from totting up the points he thought he'd got so far: best case scenario, worst case scenario and somewhere in between. Tomorrow's papers could change everything. He had to get a good night's sleep tonight so as to hit the ground running.

He sat up and ran a hand through his shoulder-length hair. He could take one of the sleeping pills he'd been prescribed for insomnia, but he didn't want to risk feeling drowsy in the morning, and anyway he was stockpiling them in case he didn't get the points and wound up doing the thing all the time to relieve the pressure.

He took a few deep breaths and cracked his knuckles. A wank wouldn't have made any difference either. Even if he did nod off afterwards, his kid sister hadn't come home yet. It was pretty much a certainty that if by some miracle he did manage to fall asleep, Keira would arrive back and start a shouting match with their parents.

They were nervous wrecks downstairs waiting for her to get in, taking turns all night to make coffee and tiptoeing into the hall for hushed calls to hospital wards, nightclubs and, Jamie was pretty certain, the morgue.

As if.

Keira was having way too much fun. She was only fourteen years old – three years younger than him – but she was completely out of control.

Their mum was a cop and dad, a teacher; if they couldn't control her, nobody could.

What his parents did for a living was another reason he was so stressed. They had this thing about sending him and Keira to private schools to give them the chances they'd never had. But it meant they'd to work every spare minute of overtime to afford the fees.

Jamie had never told them how much he hated school in the six years he'd been going there; he hadn't wanted to disappoint them. It wasn't that he'd been bullied – his height had put the rugger buggers off: he was six foot four – just that he hadn't made one real friend in all his time there. He'd never fitted in; he hated the condescending attitude to anyone different and to girls. So he'd spent every single day of every single year studying really hard to get the points he needed for college. But from tomorrow...

He knitted his fingers on the top of his scalp. The papers in physics and chemistry were his toughest subjects. If he didn't get a place in college...

Acid reflux rose in his throat and he swallowed it down, pressed his fingers into his aching eyelids. He was going to do the thing. It was the only way to stop his mind racing, get some sleep, and be fresh enough in the morning to bring his A-game to those papers. He got up, padded over to the bedroom door, pressing a hand against where it met the frame to open it quietly. He listened.

All quiet.

Jamie pulled the door open wider, wondering if his folks hadn't nodded off on the couch in front of the box – on mute so as not to disturb him. He headed onto the landing and leaned over the banister at the top of the stairs, straining to see if his dad's legs, which he could just about make out through the chink of the open sitting room door, were moving. He didn't want his parents clicking that he was up and fretting even more. They were due in work in the morning. Not that Keira cared about that.

'Jamie?'

His shoulders jumped. His mum had just emerged from the kitchen door at a blind spot in the hall and scared the bejesus out of him. His dad got up off the sofa and joined her. They both stared up at him then: his mum's eyes bloodshot, his dad's face grey with worry.

'You all right, son?' his father asked.

'Fine, just going to the bog – sorry.'

'Did you take the sleeping tablet?' his mum asked.

'Yep.' Jamie changed the subject. 'You two OK?'

His dad reached for his anorak from the coat stand and pulled it on. 'Fine, son. I'm just going to pop out to pick your sister up. Go back to bed.'

Jamie's mum grabbed keys from the hall table. 'I'll go with you, Bill, make sure you don't fall asleep at the wheel.' She glanced back up the stairs. 'OK, Jamie?'

Jamie rubbed the sleep from his eyes. 'Do you even know where Keira is?'

His mum looked away.

His dad said, 'We won't be long.'

Jamie waited until he heard their car drive off before heading into his sister's room. It was full of the shit Keira had collected from the Saturday job she'd got in a charity shop. She called it the Dead Shop because dead people's tat kept getting dumped in cardboard boxes on the doorstep when their houses were cleared out. Jamie had been in once, had to turn around and walk out again because the smell was like his football socks drying on a radiator. Keira had blamed the clothes mountain in a room at the back of the shop, said even the old lady skirts that stank of cat piss were piled on the heap because recycled cotton was worth a fortune.

He walked his fingers through the vinyl record collection that Keira had built up which included Bowie, The Beatles, and, because Keira didn't care what people thought of her, Liberace, Perry Como, and Neil Diamond. No new additions, though.

A flare of pink caught Jamie's eye, and he reached out to touch the new feather boa draped around a proper mannequin that Keira had brought home and christened 'Sue'. Pink feathers started floating to the ground – it was falling apart.

'Douchebag' was Jamie's nickname for his sister, but even though she was a major pain in the backside, he had to admit she was pretty cool. She wasn't intimidated by being the poor relation in her posh class full of the daughters of ambassadors, a Booker-prize winning author and the fucking president. She didn't care about money, grades, or points. Keira had a practical entourage of rich bitches following her around wherever she went. Even Jamie's mate – Darren from national school – went all derpy around her, making Jamie suspect that was the real reason he still kept in touch.

Jamie pulled Keira's wardrobe door open to see what clothes she'd picked up since he'd last had a look. You couldn't pay most people to take the shit she brought home.

He reached in, pushed the clothes along, ran a hand down a new moth-ridden fur... and a pure silk, blood-red kimono. He pulled it out, held it to his cheek, exhaled as the softness touched his skin, the tension starting to flood out of his muscles.

It was like a drug, this thing he'd started doing a couple of months back.

He knew he was hooked because he hadn't been able to stop even though he wanted to stop. It was weird and fucked up, but he wasn't gay which would have been so easy. No, just to complicate things, Jamie fancied the arse off girls, especially Keira's pal, Abbey, a Gwen Stefani lookalike.

It was the pressure of the Leaving Certificate, he told himself, slipping his arms into the fabric. Once the exams were behind him, he was going to cut the queer shit out, so technically that made this time the last.

Jamie sighed, sat down at Keira's dresser and stared at himself in the mirror. Her curtains were open and streetlight flooded in.

Squirting some of his sister's foundation onto the back of his hand, he rubbed his fingertips in it and started to smear it on his face. Instantly his acne was less angry, he loved that.

He leaned forward and applied black liquid eyeliner, gave himself a kink at the corners, Amy Winehouse style. It wasn't just that the world felt like a kinder place, it was how it made him feel on the inside: softer, happier, OK in his own skin.

He glanced at the handle of Keira's underwear drawer and swallowed. He pulled it open, closed his eyes as he pushed past his sister's panties. He wasn't a pervert, he was just looking – feeling really – for something... He pulled out the fishnet tights Keira didn't wear – 'too slutty', she'd told him when he asked – because they were red. He thought them divine. He pulled his jocks off and the tights on, admiring himself in the full-length mirror after adjusting himself between his legs so there was no giveaway.

Grabbing the blonde wig off Sue, he put it on and started to sway, pretending he was in a club and nobody knew he was a bloke.

He was so mesmerised by the sexy lady dancing in front of him that he almost didn't hear it.

Jamie froze.

It sounded like someone had put a key in the front door, but that couldn't be right because his folks hadn't been gone five minutes and he hadn't heard their car coming back. Her bedroom hadn't flashed with headlights either. He peeped out Keira's window.

Relief flooded through him; he must have imagined the noise, the car wasn't in the drive.

'It's not here,' Jamie heard Keira say in the hall.

If he left the room now, his sister, and who ever she was talking to, would have a clear view up of him at the top of the stairs.

'You're going to get me into trouble,' a man with a Northern Ireland accent said in a turned-on voice.

Jamie's heart started to race. He peeped out the crack in Keira's door. They were on the way up: Keira and the Northie – some old, bald geezer groping his kid sister.

Fuck, fuck, fuck.

They were going to come in to her room, find him like this. He'd never live it down. Keira being a slapper who'd brought some middle-aged fuck home would be completely eclipsed by what he'd been doing.

His heart raced. They were nearly at the top of the stairs.

Diving under Keira's bed, Jamie put a hand over his mouth. Keira's door creaked all the way open.

'What will you say if they come back?' the man said.

Jamie stared at the size twelves, approximately four feet from his face. He'd only ever seen steel-capped shoes like that before on bouncers.

'I showed you the car driving off,' Keira said, her bottle green uniform skirt falling to the floor. 'They'll be looking for me in Bray. It will take them half an hour to get there and half an hour to get back.'

Keira's blouse fell next... and then her bra. Jamie screwed his eyes shut.

The springs overhead bounced towards his face, stopping only a matter of inches short. He had to do something, to stop this...

Steelcaps nudged the backs of his shoes off with his toes before his feet disappeared from sight.

Jamie had to turn his head sideways quickly so the mattress dipping dramatically all of a sudden wouldn't connect.

'Turn over,' Steelcaps said.

Keira sniffed. Jamie gagged behind his hand and swallowed it back.

'Is there anyone else in the house?' Steelcaps demanded.

'Just my brother but he's got exams tomorrow and has to take pills. He can't sleep without them.'

Steelcaps groaned with pleasure.

Jamie grimaced. His sister was only fourteen. This was rape. He had to do something. He had to tell this bollox to fuck off. He had to batter him. He had to ring his folks. He had to stop this...

Tears started to roll down Jamie's face. He'd die before he'd let anyone find out about the thing.

It only took around three minutes for the pervert to grunt like a pig and get off the bed but it felt like three hours. Jamie watched as the man's hand swept up his kacks, a ring on his wedding finger.

He gasped at the sight of his own boxers still on the floor. If Keira saw them, found him here, he wouldn't just be a weirdo for the rest of his life, he'd be a Peeping Tom or worse: sick in the head, a deviant...

'What are you getting up for?' Steelcaps asked Keira as her feet landed on the floor. She still had her white knee socks on. 'I can let myself out.'

Jamie so wanted to punch the shit out of him for talking to his little sister like that. She was only a kid.

'You promised E for me and my friends, remember?' Keira asked.

'Tonight?' Steelcaps answered, sounding pissed off.

'It'll have to be,' Keira said, her voice all chirpy just like a little kid negotiating pocket money from their old man.

Why couldn't she see how horrible this asshole was?

'Cos after tonight I'm going to be grounded so—'

'I'll have to go back to the club,' Steelcaps complained.

'No probs,' Keira said, zipping her skirt on. 'Oh – where's Sue's hair?'

Jamie's heart seized.

'What?' the man asked.

'Sue – my mannequin – her wig's gone.'

Jamie thought the game was up but then he heard something bang down.

'Happy?' Keira asked, her feet planted beside the pervert's near her bedroom door.

He grunted something back. There was a clunking sound and then Jamie saw their feet traipse out of the room, heard them carry on down the stairs.

After waiting until he'd heard the front door open and close, Jamie scrambled out. He knelt on Keira's bed and peeped out her window, saw her walking away from the house with her paedophile boyfriend. It was the last time he saw her do that. Keira never came home.

1—ALMOST TEN YEARS LATER

It had taken almost ten years for *The Night Show* to persuade me to do an interview about my missing daughter on primetime TV. Every year, in the run up to the anniversary of Keira's disappearance, they'd send a shaky intern to my door claiming it was their first door knock. When that didn't work, some slick exec would call on the phone to tell me how much the Irish nation cared about Keira, how much they wanted me to see things from their point of view, that she was 'everyone's daughter'. Every year, I'd slam the door closed, the phone down. But in three days it would be ten years since I'd seen my baby. I was scared I'd wake up on that day with no hope left. I needed a new lead.

Ten years.

I put my arms out like a zombie as some guy with earphones around his neck opened the top button of my blouse. He put his hand down and pulled a wire through.

'You mustn't rustle or move, Helen,' he warned as he pinned a tiny mic to my buttonhole.

Keira's face grinned back at me on a giant screen behind him; it was the one taken on Bray Head a couple of weeks before she'd vanished. Her button nose was crinkled with laughter because she'd just been drenched by a wave that had turned her blonde braids frizzy with brine.

At least they'd chosen a picture of her that was real, I told myself, unlike the usual one the newspapers went for, her hair GHD'd to within an inch of its life.

'Dermot will be with you in a sec,' Wendy – the show's producer, wearing knee-high jackboots – said as the sound guy put the earphones on and walked away.

She twisted the cap off a bottle of sparkling water on my side of the presenter's desk. I watched her add a dribble to a waiting glass, lean back to examine it, and repeat several times until she'd got the water to the exact one-third mark.

'He's just grabbing a quick bite of lunch,' Wendy continued, 'hope it's not putting you out too much.'

She'd been a bit snippy with me ever since I'd refused point blank to do the interview that night on the live show. Prior to that she'd kept patting my hand like a nurse would an injured child.

I hadn't pushed for a pre-record at lunchtime because of nerves; I'd promised one of my families – the Smiths – that I'd have dinner with them after their daughter's killer was sentenced later. I worked as a Family Liaison Officer, a sort of go-between for an incident room and those left behind to pick up the pieces after the worst happened. The man who'd killed their daughter Anna had been found not guilty of murder but guilty of manslaughter, which meant the difference between a mandatory life sentence and the possibility of a suspended one. The Smiths were scared how they'd react if he got off, so I'd promised to bring the news. Wendy knew all this, but it hadn't stopped her asking: 'Would this tragic girl's poor parents mind awfully if you rearranged?'

I watched as Jamie – my son – and my husband, Bill, filed into the empty audience seats in the front row.

A young male with pointy shoes and hair gelled into the shape of a ski slope scuttled over towards me. He knelt down on his hunkers, presumably so we were at the same eye level. I wondered if body language was a module on media courses nowadays.

'Hi, we spoke on the phone. I'm Ted, the researcher, great to meet you. I just want to tell you that if Dermot raises his eyebrows while looking at you, you need to talk about something else.'

'I'm here to talk about Keira.'

'Of course,' he smiled, 'but if you're talking about, say, Keira's last known movements and you see Dermot's eyebrows go up you need to move on to something else like various lines of enquiry or whatever?'

'Can't Dermot just interrupt me?' I asked, tetchily.

'He'd look insensitive, though,' Ted explained, tilting his head like a dog trying to understand. 'Everything's so much larger than life on screen.'

A make-up girl flurried up with a brush swept in powder and started to dust my face. 'Sorry, you're like an oil slick on camera.'

The man of the moment arrived at that point – like a drunken giraffe in need of a dose of Ritalin.

'So good to finally meet you, Helen,' Dermot Skeffington-Walsh said, shaking my hand effusively. 'Is it OK if I call you Helen? I'm so sorry about what you've been through. You have no idea how many years I've wanted to hear your story. So many people go missing, but so few capture the imagination the way Keira has. Well – she's everyone's daughter, don't you think? The good news is our show's TAMs are through the roof so if anyone can find her, *The Night Show* can.'

I drew a breath.

He sat down, and the make-up girl moved to him, waving a can of hairspray about his head. I coughed as Dermot stared at a camera hurtling towards him along a miniature railway track.

'We're just filling the front few rows with staff members right now,' Dermot explained. 'That way, when we pan to your family members, it will segue with tonight's audience.'

Another cameraman started waving frantically like an air traffic controller at him. Dermot turned seamlessly to face him, 'I'll start with asking you to bring me back to the night Keira vanished, Helen,' he said, his face turned at least ninety degrees away from mine, 'what you remember, however upsetting – we can cut the unnecessary stuff afterwards – and then we'll move on to the investigation, suspects, and the appeal for new information. How does that sound?'

I shrugged. No pitch would ever have been enough to persuade me to barter my daughter's memory as if it was some kind of commodity. I needed the public's help.

Dermot glanced at the colleagues, whose slumped shoulders suggested they had been sequestered from their lunch breaks.

A floor manager jabbed an index finger at the seats they were to sit in, presumably to give the impression of a full house.

Dermot rubbed his hands together, 'OK, let's get this show on the road.' After tweaking his tie and clearing his throat, his expression grew morose. 'Now, ladies and gentlemen, we are all familiar with the name Keira Chambers. She is Ireland's most well-known missing person. Her face has been on the front of so many newspapers it has become iconic.

'Keira was fourteen years old when she went to school one day and never came home. Tonight *The Night Show* asks why this case in particular means so much to us. Other teenage girls haven't come home in this country, but Keira's is the case we remember.

'Is it her beauty, the fact that she came from such a safe, south Dublin suburb that resonates? Is it the fact that her parents were such respectable, decent people, people like you and I, that this tragedy still catches us in the throat?'

His voice went down a notch. 'Is it possible that the country was so awash with cash in 2006 that Keira's disappearance reminds us of our own moral bankruptcy a decade ago?'

I reached for the glass of water and gulped it back.

Dermot paused momentously and then swivelled suddenly to look at another camera: 'Please put your hands together for Keira's mum, Helen Chambers, who is going to tell the nation for the first time what the last ten years have been like for her family in another world exclusive for *The Night Show*.'

Canned applause filled the studio. A cameraman hurtled towards me. I glanced at Bill, his handsome face gaunt under the studio lights.

'Helen,' Dermot said, snapping me back to the moment. 'Tell me about Keira. Who was she? What was she like? How do you remember your lost daughter?'

I shifted on the seat; spotted the sound guy putting his hands on his head in the distance.

'Well – Keira was my youngest, and she was always the baby of our house,' I said. 'She wasn't just beautiful, she was very, very bright. She was reading by the age of three, and really anything she put her mind to, she did brilliantly. She was an amazing dancer and singer and a terrific artist. She was astonishingly creative, looking back, and she had the most brilliant sense of humour. She was also very, very kind. Sometimes I think too kind. And she absolutely loved children—'

Dermot's eyebrows were almost touching his hairline.

'So Keira was just the light of our lives really,' I said.

Dermot shook his head sadly, 'That bright, effervescent light that was her essence, which you have so poetically described, went out on June 12th, 2006. Will you take us through what you remember about that day?' He glanced at his notes.

I swallowed. 'So Keira went to school in Bray as per normal,' I said. 'It was a Monday morning—'

Dermot reached for the carafe of water and offered to refill the third I'd just drained. I put the glass down on the floor beside the chair out of his reach and continued, 'And when she wasn't home by four-thirty p.m., I tried calling her phone, but it had been confiscated by one of the teachers earlier in the day and rang out. I went to the school at five-thirty p.m. to see if anyone knew where she was. Some of the girls still there thought she had gone to Eddie Rocket's restaurant so I went there. In the restaurant, I met—'

Dermot's eyebrows went up dramatically again. I looked away, we'd never nailed down Keira's last movements. 'I met a waitress who remembered Keira had been there after school and I established from the waitress's description that she'd been with friends: Abbey Martin and Rachel Knowles.

So, I—'

'So what time did you report Keira a missing person after she failed to come home on the last bus?' Dermot asked quickly.

'We did that at nine the following morning, the thirteenth of June,' I said.

'Why so long?'

'Well... I... we—,' I glanced at Bill and he nodded back, '...we just believed Keira would come home, eventually.'

'She'd stayed out all night before, without clearing it with you and not answering her phone, at fourteen years old?'

I blew out a spurt of air; gave a single nod.

Dermot banged his question cards on the table to form a tidy stack. 'She was very young for that, wasn't she?'

'Yes.'

'Do you think, looking back, that you gave her too much freedom?'

I sighed; it wasn't like my fourteen-year-old daughter had ever been allowed to stay out all night. Allowed hadn't come into it.

In any event, Dermot was blooded. 'Doesn't that tell us something about a certain time in our country's history?'

'I'm not sure I understand the question—'

'That we had no limits? That we believed even our children were entitled to live to excess?'

I opened my mouth to answer but, again, didn't get the chance.

He leaned across his desk, 'I'm sorry to have to ask you this, Helen,' he said, not sounding remotely sorry. 'But have you ever thought that Keira might have been a victim of Pickup-Rick?' The bunny fingers he'd made hung in the air.

'Unlikely,' I said. Nobody knew if Rick actually even existed. The media had given the moniker to the person presumed responsible for the disappearance of two hitch-hiking women.

No one materialised from the wings. 'Those cases occurred in the south of Ireland,' I went on, 'and the second unfortunate lady's case was almost twenty years before Keira vanished.' I shook my head, 'There were no sightings of anyone matching Keira's description hitch-hiking.'

That didn't stop Dermot from speculating. 'But you live in Sally's Pass? The highest village in Ireland is practically the middle of nowhere. How else would she have got home?'

I studied my hands. When the children were young, Sally's Pass had seemed like the perfect place to bring up a family. It was within commuting distance of Dublin but a million miles away. It was a place of stunning natural beauty and, as a result, a magnet for *Tour de France* style cyclists, camper vans, and film-makers dragging props like Viking boats to the loughs. Even in the winter months the mountain rescue helicopter constantly whirred overhead because of the amount of people who ignored the 'Danger – Impassable' signs at the foot of Devil's Elbow – the mountain Sally's Pass was perched on. But after Keira vanished, everything that had been a novelty became hostile and remote. I'd stare into the windscreens of rental cars where steam hot spots rose from flasks and shudder at the faces of strangers staring back.

I'd look for chinks in the curtains of camper vans and try to peer through them.

I came to regard the vast, impenetrable mountains as alien and hostile, the perfect place to dump a body.

Dermot stood up suddenly. 'But life marches on, as it must...' he said. The camera moved with him as he paced towards the front row.

'How are you, Bill?'

My husband sighed.

'I always think that the role of father and provider is dealt a death blow if a child goes missing. Is that the case?'

Bill put a hand across his eyes. The cameraman moved closer. I stood up quickly, the sound pack hitting the floor and starting to trail after me as I took a step.

Wendy raced towards me. 'We're nearly there, Helen,' she whispered, 'sit down, please.'

When I didn't, she started to pat the air between us frantically. 'But we haven't done the appeal for information yet.'

Dermot glanced over his shoulder to see what was going on.

'I'm sorry,' Bill said, smearing his wet face with his giant palm. 'It's just... you're right Dermot. It's been very difficult.'

I sat down slowly.

'Keira was my princess,' Bill continued. 'I could always fix things for her when she was little, you know? But not this. Not this.' He put his head down and started to sob.

A smile twitched on the producer's lips.

Dermot put a leg up on the bench separating the audience from the studio and leaned on it. 'And Jamie, you were Keira's only brother. Tell us your last memory of Keira please?'

Jamie shrugged. 'Her walking out of the house, down our street in the middle of the night.'

I glanced at my husband. Bill had clocked our son's mistake too, and he caught my eye, giving me a barely perceptible frown.

'Join us after the break,' Dermot said as the show's jingle filled the air.

The floor manager motioned by slicing and slashing the air that nobody was to move yet under any circumstances. But that didn't stop Jamie from standing and pacing towards the red-lit exit sign.

Louise Sharland's first novel *Vigil* was shortlisted for the *Daily Mail* crime writing competition. *Vengeance Street*, about a Probation Officer drawn into a dark world of violence and vigilante justice, is set in her home city of Plymouth and addresses complex issues such as masculine identity and domestic violence.

niklou.sharland@blueyonder.com

Vengeance Street

I glance down at my mobile phone and smile. It hasn't taken me long to find the three young men huddled behind the bus shelter passing a joint between them. Incredible what you can do with the 'Find My Friends' app on an iPhone.

I inch closer, pretending to be reading the bus timetable but really focusing my attention on the tallest of the three: he is tall, well built, with shiny hair and a 3D tattoo of a crucifix that edges its way past his shirt cuff and on to the back of his hand.

I check the photograph that has been messaged to me and nod. The only difference being that he is dressed up for a night out: crisp white shirt, black jeans and leather espadrilles with designer logos that reflect the headlights of oncoming cars.

I check my watch – still early. From experience I know it will be another hour or so, another joint or two; a trip to the off-licence for some cheap rum and a bottle of Diet Coke.

I cross the road, settle myself into the shadow of a tall oak and wait.

It is nearly eleven by the time they decide to stumble their way to the harbour front. The bank holiday weather means the crowds are out in droves; the queue outside The Dolphin winds its way past the chippie three shops away. They march to the front, past the doorman, without looking back. By the time I get inside they're finishing their first round. The shiny-haired boy says something to his friends; they all laugh and head towards the men's toilets.

'A long line of coke would make that frosty Stella taste even better,' I mutter.

A few minutes later they're back, ordering a row of tequila shots and more Stella. Not a penny changes hands.

Nice for some.

For the next half-hour, I watch them ricochet between mellow and hyper, jostling the Chinese students who are quietly introducing themselves to a pint of scrumpy, or eyeing up the locals who have made it in for the two-for-one ladies' night.

I'm just thinking about leaving when I notice a small blonde with dark slashes for eyebrows struggling her way to the bar. The boy marks her approach with a grin. He nods to his mates and downs his shot. The girl, not even half his size, smiles shyly as he pulls up a bar stool and helps her on, all the time giving her a greedy once-over. It's as if I'm watching one of those wildlife programmes where the cameraman films the shark circling the sea lion. No matter what the outcome, human intervention is forbidden. Nature, after all, must be allowed to take its course.

Outside, the breeze feels cool against my neck as I follow them into the darkness. Streetlights glimmer in the harbour opposite the cobblestoned alley where the boy leads her, where there are no cameras. Her back is against the wall and the boy is pushing against her, slipping one hand between her thighs and yanking up the fake leather miniskirt with the other.

'Don't!' she cries.

'What do you mean don't?'

I watch as she struggles, tries to lift her arms to push him away.

'Stop it!' She sounds frightened, like a little girl.

'Come on baby,' the boy laughs. He presses his mouth against hers, holds her against the wall with one hand and with the other starts to undo his trousers. She tears at his designer shirt. A button pops and spirals to the ground, bouncing off the uneven stone.

'Bitch!' He gives the girl a shake and slams her back against the wall, her head hitting the bricks with a soft thud.

Behind me, I hear footsteps – two long shadows either side. I lift a finger in warning.

'Wait,' I whisper. 'The fruit of the spirit is in forbearance and self-control.'

In the alleyway the girl is fighting back.

'Get off me, you bastard!' she screams, and in a moment of inspired desperation stabs her stiletto heel into the toe of the boy's espadrille. I hear him yell, see him stumble, and then to my surprise watch as the girl pushes him so hard that he topples backwards onto the cobbles.

Good girl.

Kicking away her heels she runs barefoot into the night, her sobs echoing the cries of ever present seagulls.

Next to me the two shadows chuckle.

'Like a girl wif spirit,' says one.

'Don't take no shite,' says the other.

They're like two hunting dogs waiting for the signal. I turn towards them, give them a nod.

'Cheers, boss.'

'Make it tidy,' I say, 'not like last time.'

Ahead of them the boy is struggling to his feet, a shaky silhouette. Two shadows move towards him.

'Like to pick on 'elpless girls?' one of them says.

'Make you feel like a man?' says the other.

'Fuck off,' the boy replies, dusting dirt off his skinny jeans.

'That's no way to talk to your elders,' says one.

'Your betters,' says the other.

'Get the fuck out of my way,' the boy says, trying to push past them.

The first punch hits him on the jaw and sends him flying. His chin smashes onto the cobblestones, his front teeth shatter. There is a kick in the chest, then another; the sound of splintering ribs, red foam on his lips. He begins crawling his way towards the harbour, small mewing noises coming from his ruined and bloody mouth. Strong hands lift him by the armpits, drag him towards the light.

'Like the water, do we?' says one.

CHAPTER ONE

It was eight-thirty am and Claire Freshwater was making her way up the stairs towards the second-floor reception area of Devonport House, the modern four-storey building in the centre of Plymouth that housed the National Probation Service. Pushing open the double doors, she stepped into what, for all intents and purposes, looked like a GP's surgery waiting room. Two rows of interlinked seating covered in faded tartan material curved their way towards a small table dotted with discarded leaflets. Above that was a noticeboard promoting a range of useful information and upcoming events:

Sexual Health Clinic every Thursday 2-5pm at The Lighthouse Centre
Struggling with substance misuse?
Anxiety and depression getting you down?

In the lower right-hand corner was a newspaper clipping that read:

Homemade Turkey Masala.
A great way to use up Christmas leftovers!

It was May.

Just ahead was the reception desk. That was where any resemblance to a doctor's surgery ended. The large built-in counter reached to chest height and was plastered with a large laminated sign that read:

Please do not use abusive, profane or racist language when dealing with National Probation Services staff. Any threatening language or behaviour will be taken seriously, and police will immediately be called.

Above the desk, a blockade of reinforced glass rose to ceiling height. Any communication between visitors and those interned behind the barricade was via a small opening – wide enough to slip through an A4 envelope but not a fist.

It was still early, and the waiting area was empty. Claire gave a quick wave to the two colleagues who manned the desk and punched her security code into the adjoining door and entered what was jokingly referred to by staff as the grey mile. A long corridor stretched out before her like a monochrome road. Immediately to her right was a pod-like interview room constructed of strengthened glass. She knew that inside there were two panic alarms, one by the door and one secreted under the desk. There was also a 360° CCTV camera and a live audio feed. This was where some of the most dangerous sex offenders in the country were interviewed. A card had been slipped into a plastic frame on the door; it read *Freshwater 09:00 hours*. Claire sighed and carried on down the corridor to the main office. Another keypad-secured door led into the large open-plan office.

'Morning,' called Claire's case assistant, Ginny Lowe. She was pouring herself a cup of coffee from a large cafetière. She held it high. 'There's enough for two.' Claire smiled gratefully and made her way to her desk.

'Sarah's case file,' said Ginny, handing Claire a mug of steaming coffee and a manila coloured file folder with a large, wrap-around security ribbon. She lowered her voice and leaned in closer. 'She's been signed off for two weeks with stress, but odds are she won't be back for months.'

'I just wish she'd told us she was struggling.'

'You're already at your maximum caseload,' said Ginny, her forehead creased with concern. 'Are you sure you can handle another one?'

'Don't think I have much choice,' said Claire. The manila folder felt heavy in her hand. 'Is it the chap I've been reading about in *The Herald*?'

'His previous was pretty awful,' said Ginny. 'Tied his wife to the bed and—'

'I remember.' She placed the envelope on the desk in front of her and carefully unravelled the crimson bow. She knew that inside was an eight-page offender risk management form which provided key intelligence on the offender. Claire had seen hundreds in her ten-year career and was now adept at speed-reading through most of them. Good thing too, as it was less than twenty minutes until her appointment. In the bottom right-hand corner of the file someone had scrawled the letters *DV* in pencil. She felt her heart rate quicken, took a breath to steady herself. For most of her career,

Claire had specialised in domestic violence and sexual offence cases. Her work had been highly commended as far north as Bristol. There had even been talk of her heading up a specialist unit in Exeter.

'It was all going so smoothly,' she muttered, before slicing the paper seal on the report with her thumbnail. She took a sip of coffee, sat down and began to read.

Perpetrator: *Mr William (Billy) Vale.*
D.O.B: *27 January 1982, 36 years old.*
Ethnicity: *White British.*
Place of residence: *Flat 4, 15 Batter Place, Stonehouse, Plymouth.*

Overview of Index Office:
On the evening of 7th January, Mr Vale, after having a verbal altercation with his wife Nicole, struck her in the face and punched her in the abdomen and ribs, incapacitating her. He then dragged her by the hair into the marital bedroom where he tied her to the bedposts with her tights and proceeded to burn various parts of her body, including her genital area, with her straightening irons, which he had bought her for Christmas.

Claire gave a little huff of frustration at the received sentence of four years' imprisonment – one year suspended – and then a silent nod of comprehension when she discovered who the presiding judge had been. She glanced at her watch to see if she still had time to log on to her secure laptop where she could access more detailed information, all of which would be used to determine the level of risk the perpetrator posed to themselves and to others. Once input into the database the various categories of risk, including causing serious harm, escape and absconding, as well as risk to the public, would be calculated and then presented as a hazard score of one to ten. There had been a training session only a few months ago, in which a baby-faced facilitator had insisted that his software programme could provide an accurate prediction of risk of reoffending within a margin of 1.5%. She could still remember his look of stunned incredulity when the training room erupted into gales of laughter.

'Of course, it's all down to a simple mathematical calculation,' muttered Claire.

She skipped to the last page of the form to discover why Billy Vale had been recalled to probation, and why she would be interviewing him in approximately two minutes' time.

Incident that instigated recall to probation services:

11 May, 19:00 hours.

Mrs Vale returned to her flat on Sedgemoor Street after her shift at the Sunnyvale Care Home on Nepean Avenue to discover a series of Post-it notes had been placed on her front door by her ex-husband Mr William Vale. These notes included statements such as 'I'll love you forever', pleas for forgiveness and requests to have access to his four-year-old daughter Jasmine. In these notes Mr Vale was now 'seeking to make amends for my sins.' Mrs Vale was understandably distressed. This matter is currently being investigated by Mrs Vale's legal team with a view to extending his current restraining order.

'Not very bright is our Billy,' whispered Claire, too annoyed to put her unconscious bias training into practice. There were a few hastily scribbled notes and a lot of unsigned paperwork. It was clear that her colleague Sarah had been under a lot a pressure and hadn't been coping.

'Why didn't you talk to me?' whispered Claire. She was just making notes of her own when her telephone rang.

'Yes?'

'William Vale for you.'

'Thanks Hannah, I'll be out in a sec.'

Claire took another sip of coffee, picked up the file and headed for reception.

CHAPTER TWO

The high-risk interview room had a particular smell. A mixture of sweat, burnt plastic and used fat from the tapas bar across the street. Claire kept a tiny bottle of Neal's Yard Mint & Lemon breath spray in her back pocket and often gave it a little spritz just before she started an interview.

'What's that smell?'

She had collected William Vale from reception and was waiting for him to take his seat when he spoke.

'Good morning, Mr Vale. My name is Claire Freshwater and I will be your temporary Offender Manager for the next few weeks. Please have a seat.'

'What's that fucking smell?'

Claire decided she would take a few moments to let silence do its job. The trick was not to give them the opportunity to get a handle on you. Reacting too quickly – a raised eye, a tightening of the voice – was always a mistake. It made them think they could work you, push your buttons. The trick was to remain neutral, calm and, when necessary, absolutely quiet.

She waited until he was seated, and she had counted ten ticks from the clock on the wall behind his head before clearing her throat.

'Mr Vale, I'd like to talk to you about what happened a few days ago.'

'Sort of smells like mint humbugs.'

Claire moved effortlessly and systematically to step two: the unimpressed stare, held it until he blinked.

'Mr Vale. Billy. May I call you Billy?'

'Don't give a shit what you call me.'

She gave a slow, close-mouthed smile, waited and then glanced at her watch.

'Well that makes things a bit easier then, doesn't it, Billy?'

His eyes narrowed but he did not reply.

'As I mentioned when I collected you from reception, we've only got half an hour together this morning. I would suggest that the best way forward would be for us to focus on what happened a few days ago and how best we can deal with it immediately and effectively. Otherwise, you will most likely see yourself back in the nick by lunchtime.' Billy's shoulders sagged almost imperceptibly.

She opened the case file. 'Well now, there seems to be plenty of information about what happened: reports from the police, social services, solicitors. There are even statements from half a dozen people in the flats across the street.' His look hardened and suddenly Claire could see the danger in him. The short fuse, raised fist and unending need to make the pain last.

'I've got a few questions about that myself,' he said, and, bending down, began rifling through a shopping bag full of papers he had brought with him. It gave Claire the chance to study him more closely. She knew from his file that he was thirty-six, originally from Rotherham, and had spent most of his teenage years in care. There was a list of minor offences on his sheet: petty theft, common assault, possession, but nothing that had earned him a spell inside, and certainly nothing to suggest that he would one day tie his partner to a bed frame and torture her while their three-year-old daughter slept peacefully in the room next door. He was small, maybe five foot six, but with a wiry frame that suggested suppressed energy and violence. His hair was close-cut, and he had very blue eyes. Claire openly acknowledged her bias, derived in part from the report that categorised Billy Vale as high risk, but there was something else, something less tangible. After ten years in the probation service she tended to trust her instincts, so why hadn't they served her better nine months earlier when everything went so wrong? For a moment her confidence faltered.

'As I didn't actually have any physical contact with her.'

'Pardon?'

She watched Billy's face harden, could almost hear him growl.

'I said "as I didn't actually have any physical contact with her". Are you listening to me or what?'

'Yes, of course.'

Never apologise.

She returned quickly to what she knew best, paperwork and procedure.

'The thing is, Billy, that the restraining order is part and parcel of your licence. The rules by which you have to abide in order to stay out of prison state clearly that you are not allowed to be within a five-mile radius of Miss Tanner, her daughter, family or any other associated friends or relatives.'

'It's *my* daughter,' he hissed, '*my* wife.'

'Ex-wife!' snapped Claire.

Shit, shit, shit.

She watched him sit back, fold his arms across his chest and zone out. She was going to have to get this back on course and quick. Her boss Simon Ellison had told her before going in this morning that the holding cells at Charles Cross Police Station were full and that a security alert at Dartmoor Prison meant any new intakes would be driven thirty-three miles to HMP Channingswood in Newton Abbott. To top it all off, most of the prisoner transport was booked or out of commission. Her remit had been clear, if possible and appropriate keep Billy Vale out of jail while making sure his risk stats were below 5%. Shame she had forgotten to bring her calculator with her.

'Look Billy,' she gave him an apologetic smile. Let him think he had her on the back foot for a bit. 'Let's start again, shall we?' His gaze did not soften, body language did not change. 'Now the thing is, before this incident on Wednesday you had a pretty good record. You've got a steady job as a general labourer—'

'Bricklayer.'

'Pardon?'

'I'm a brickie not a labourer, though I do painting and decorating jobs as well.'

'Oh yes, of course,' she made a show of looking at his file. Getting some of their details wrong was a technique she often used to get them talking. 'Not knowing the difference is probably why I've still got those massive cracks in the back wall of my house.' Claire shook her head and tried to look confused. 'I mean the last chap who came to price it up *called* himself a bricklayer, but he didn't really seem to know what he was doing. He said it might need a complete rebuild.'

'Load of bullshit.'

'What?'

'If it was subsidence, which it sounds like, then he'd be talking about digging up and underpinning it. Still a pricy job but not as much as rebuilding an entire wall. Sounds like you were being taken for a ride, love.'

She had him.

'Well thanks, Billy. I'll keep that in mind.'

Another smile.

'So you've been out of prison for nearly eighteen months and living in Plymouth without a single incident. I see you've completed all the programmes: *Building Better Relationships, Domestic Violence Perpetrator.* How did you find those?'

'All right.'

'Good attendance and excellent participation according to these notes. You even became a peer mentor on one of them. That's pretty impressive.' Leaning forward, she rested her chin on her hand. 'So, what happened?' There was something there, she could tell, could almost see it. 'Was there someone else? Had Nicole started seeing someone else?'

'I don't know what all the fuss was about,' said Billy, shaking his head. 'A few Post-it notes on her front door and all hell breaks loose.'

'You frightened her, Billy.'

'Didn't mean to.'

'What *did* you mean to do?'

He paused, studied the wall above her head.

'I just wanted to say sorry.'

Claire stared at him. 'Sorry?'

'Sorry for what I'd done, for hurting her, messin' up what we had.'

The next question came to her without thinking.

'What made you decide to do that, to say sorry I mean?'

He looked at her then, held her gaze. This time she was the first to blink. He paused, using the silence, Claire realised, to determine if *she* was worth confiding in.

'I found my way back.'

'Back?'

'To Jesus.'

It was the moment that would make or break their relationship and any chance Claire had of clocking up Billy Vale as a successful outcome. If she responded too cynically, in a *you're taking the piss* kind of way, she would lose him. If she was overly sincere and he *was* taking the piss, all her credibility would go down the drain. She wasn't quite sure what to say next, so replied with what she truly felt.

'Now that's *very* interesting.'

Then Billy Vale did something completely unexpected. He smiled.

'That's not what most people say.' He rubbed his hand across the bristles on his chin. 'They think I've lost it or that I'm winding them up.'

'When you say returned...'

'Not to that Catholic bullshit, just,' he indicated to the file folder which summarised his life story in forty pages, 'a small, non-denominational community church. Worship, prayer and forgiveness, that's all I'm after.' He leaned forward, his elbows almost touching hers. 'Look Claire, I know what I am. I'm a hard, cruel bastard. A loser who's spent most of his life taking his shit out on the rest of the world and taking it out hard. I hurt my wife, lost my daughter and spent three years in prison. I didn't expect sympathy or understanding from anyone, but when I found my way back, well, that changed everything.'

In her ten years as a probation officer Claire had rarely had a conversation like this so early in the interview process. It usually took weeks or months, if it ever happened at all. She wasn't quite sure what to say next, so defaulted, as usual, to process. 'And your voluntary work?'

'I help out at the church.'

'Help out?'

Billy gave her a look like she was a relic, when in truth she was only two years older than him. 'I show up, clean up, build up, do whatever they need doing.' He sat up a little bit straighter. 'I helped to build the new pre-school.' Claire nodded and made a few notes in the file. 'They've all been really good to me, everyone at the church. They've offered support, guidance,' he cleared his throat as if the next bit was proving difficult, 'counselling and such.'

'That's great, Billy. I'm pleased for you, but why—'

'Mess it all up by leaving a note on my ex's door telling her I love her and asking her to forgive me?'

'Yes. Why?'

'I. Don't. Know.'

She turned the page to reread his statement after his arrest.

'But she *was* seeing someone else, wasn't she?'

There was a pause and Claire realised he was deciding whether or not he would trust her. 'Yeah,' he said finally. 'Me mate Ozzy saw her with a bloke at Prezzo.'

'And did you really think that leaving those Post-it notes on her front door would change anything?'

Billy shook his head in dejection. 'It was sincere,' he said and, lifting his hands in subjugation, whispered, 'I was seeking forgiveness, still am.'

In the distance a slow wail of a police siren gained momentum as it neared Devonport House. Claire glanced absent-mindedly out the window and watched as a squad car sped past the building and towards the harbour front. 'Forgiveness or not Billy, it was very lucky that you didn't have any actual contact with her. Because if you had you would be in holding cells right now, waiting to go back to Dartmoor.'

'Don't you think I know that?'

Claire returned to the last few pages of his file which she had unthinkingly marked up with Post-it notes less than an hour before. Feeling her cheeks begin to glow she quickly peeled away the strips of neon-coloured paper and slipped them into her pocket. She heard Billy clear his throat and when she looked up saw that he had a wide, good-natured grin on his face. She found herself smiling in return. For a few brief seconds there were no crimes, victims, convictions or prisons. There were just two people smiling.

'Well,' said Claire, returning to professional mode. 'It looks like you have quite a few prominent character witnesses. Your church pastor, local GP.'

'I really haven't put a foot wrong since I've been outside.'

'Aside from two days ago, of course.' He gave a defeated sigh, let his head fall back against the chair behind him and covered his face with his hands. Claire closed the file and cupped her chin thoughtfully. 'The thing is Billy, you messed up, and you messed up big time, but you didn't have any contact, and as soon as you realised what you'd done you handed yourself into the police. It's probably those things along with your exceptional record for the last year and half, as well as the character references, that have kept you out of jail.'

He sat up suddenly and fixed her with his cobalt gaze.

'Does that mean I won't have to go back inside?'

'Well, it's still early days and you will be given a court date...'

'But?'

'Considering the nature of the breach, no direct contact with Nicole or Jasmine and your recent history, I would be hoping for a medium-level community order.'

'Just talk English, will you!'

'If it goes your way, and I hope it does, you'd be looking at a fine, supervision and maybe a return to some of the courses you've already done.' For the first time in the last half hour she saw hope in his eyes.

'I don't want to go back inside, Claire.'

Claire was continually amazed at the point in an interview when all the bullshit and bravado was stripped away and the real person emerged. Rarely were they charismatic or exciting; the Tony Sopranos or Hannibal Lecters of fiction. Normally they were sad, desperate, damaged people and it was these sorts of moments when she found it particularly challenging to maintain her professional distance.

'I don't want you to go back inside either,' she replied.

Billy sighed and gave her a *then what do I do* look and Claire knew at once that her outcome was safe. She picked up her pen and found a clear space on the interview record form.

'So, firstly, in order to ensure there are no repeat breaches and that we give you the best possible chance at your court appearance, I would like us to continue to meet regularly, at least every week for the next month. I'll try to make the appointments as late as possible but it may require you to leave work early. Will your employer be OK with that?'

Billy nodded enthusiastically. 'I'm sure he'll let me leave as long as I make up my hours.'

'Right, so we'll agree our next meeting at the end of this session. Unfortunately, due to the nature of your previous conviction, your restrictions and your recent breach of licence conditions, I am going to have to action what is called an "Assistant Chief Officer's Final Warning". Do you know what that means?'

'Think I can guess.'

'Just like it says on the tin Billy, final warning. If anything like this happens again, if you even sneeze within five miles of Nicole's flat, you will be going down, no questions asked.'

'Anything else?'

'I'd like you to revisit the *Victim Empathy* module of the *Building Better Relationships* programme. Do you still have the booklets?'

'Yeah, I guess so.'

He sounded like a bored schoolboy, like her teenage son, Jack.

'Good, we'll look at that next week. You're to maintain your employment, voluntary work, counselling sessions, and you are absolutely not to go anywhere near Nicole or Jasmine.'

Scribbling furiously on the notepad in front of her, she wrote out an action plan on the copy paper and slid it across the desk towards him.

'Your word is your bond, Billy,' she said and waited for him to sign.

Peter Sibley lives in Switzerland and is a British-born media specialist who has worked for Reuters, Greenpeace and the UK Government. He has creative and business interests in digital, moving image, radio and writing.

peter.sibley@anglomediagroup.com

Drop Dead Date

CHAPTER ONE

Everyone has a secret, they say.

I had two.

I was passed upwards through the empty atriums of the Amadori headquarters by a relay of apologetic, well-scented women who were not in the mood for small talk. Nor for Sunday evening opening hours. I appreciated their silence, and I didn't need their apologies.

But I badly needed the cash.

The women stepped quickly as if something important had shifted the solid company walls on a day of rest. Their well-trained eyes refused to comment on my faded cycle shirt or venture below my waist at the worn Lycra. No one asked me to remove the bike helmet loosely secured above my scrappy hair and beard. They just passed me quickly between them like an awkward baton with a crisp, 'It's for Mr Amadori.'

Finally, as I wondered what urgent documents required a late pick-up on a weekend, I was directed down a corridor to a wide grey service lift. I was asked to enter and press the top button. I stood alone in the dim light and felt disposed of, with relief, by my handlers. The lift remained still for a while, sighed, then ground reluctantly upwards before it stopped. It considered its decision for a few seconds then opened into hard sunlight and a breeze that took the July heat away. The roof of the oldest family company in Geneva was at the high point of the city where it could take in the view of the lake and a hundred miles of mountains. It wasn't alone. The global banks and businesses stood together here like fortified friends.

Victor Amadori, CEO and guardian of four generations of business, was standing on the edge of the roof's parapet looking into the void and urinating down on the pedestrian area below.

'Welcome,' he called, without turning around. 'Are you a man for heights?'

'Yes,' I said, standing my ground so as not to disturb his flow, 'I think I am.'

'Good,' Amadori said to the view with immaculate English. 'Only two of us left.'

Then I saw the rifle propped against the low wall as Amadori worked at the zip on his trousers. If I had turned away and walked straight back into the lift, it would have ended differently. Perhaps it was the gun that made me stay; there were plenty of businessmen who would shoot a stranger in the back. Or perhaps it was the fact that the man might jump, and I would be the only witness. Or be accused of being the guilty party. And I would be as exposed as the man on the roof.

The truth was I just needed the money.

He was a small, compact man. My height where he stood on the low wall, but almost a foot shorter if we'd been on equal ground. He wore an electric blue business suit and, above the collar, his hair was short, well cut and bristle white. Smooth, black leather shoes. Precise and pointed, close to the edge. Four or five decades of success were contained within the man's suit and his shoulders were still braced firmly against the world. He waved an insistent hand to join him, as a father might encourage a son to take a risk he will benefit from.

'Come. Come stand with me here,' Amadori said. 'Come. Look...' And he turned and fixed me with intense black eyes embedded in a smooth tan.

I could see that his face wasn't all his own. The natural life lines had been removed and a narrow fold of grey skin was visible where his face met his hair. His mouth was a tiny row of sharp, pointed teeth imprisoned by a grin.

He looked like a business doll.

'Mr Amadori?' I said, offering a tentative hand, so he had to lean towards me.

He reached down and out and took it, judged it for a second then pulled me forwards with unexpected strength. I stepped up hard, veered and then straightened in a single movement to find myself next to the small man gripping tightly onto his hand. Amadori shot a laugh at me suddenly standing there with him then looked up to the sky, removed his hand and directed it across the old city rooftops. I followed his pointed finger to a flock of grey, wheeling birds which circled and dipped and lifted to some unknown set of rules.

'I've been watching them. And I've got it.' Amadori beamed, as if he had discovered how easy it was to put two and two billion together and make five. 'I've found the leader.'

The flock of city pigeons raced in wide graceful arcs, shifting between layers of height but consistently circling.

'See. There, there!' Amadori shouted.

I blinkered my eyes against the monochrome sky.

'That one! Blacker and whiter than the others. In the middle. There! Now at the back. Look. Now above!'

I couldn't see which one he meant. The birds were too similar for anyone to care, and I couldn't spot any leadership.

I just wanted to get off the wall.

'You see. You see! It dips a wing or lifts its head. It speeds up a little. It lifts above the others. Or it drops below.' He stared at me to make sure I understood. 'But look! It never rushes to the front. So subtle. So perfect.' Amadori clapped his hands and lifted onto his toes. 'And watch, watch. All the others follow!'

His body twitched and his eyes sparkled with the guarantee of a new religion. But I couldn't share his vision. I had met too many men like him in a previous life, and I was no longer the conversion type. I suspected Amadori found a new belief every day. The kind of man who traded his own passion against others' lack of it. Or bullied those who couldn't keep up with the cause.

It was time to make my escape. I made a move to step down from the wall.

'Stay with me, now,' Amadori said, tight-lipped, 'and pass me the gun.'

I paused as he locked his eyes with mine. I counted to ten. Best play safe when you're on a high wall, I told myself, so I leant down slowly and did as I was asked. Amadori grabbed the gun from me and in a single move placed it against his shoulder and pointed the barrel at my face.

I didn't move. I didn't raise my hands.

'The drop dead date,' said Amadori with the gravity of a larger man, 'is this Friday at five.'

The birds circled low across the rooftops, then rose and rounded up towards where we stood. Amadori flicked his eyes away from me towards them, then directed the gun away from my face and took sight down the barrel, tracking the flock as it lofted high above the Amadori building. He fired four times. Each time with a sharp crack. I followed the birds into the direct sun. Nothing. No feathers, no descending mess, no impact.

'Take it. Take it. Your go!' Amadori cried. 'Shoot!'

He pushed the gun towards me and I squinted the brightness out of my eyes and took it, relieved to be in control of something. I lifted the gun and aimed vaguely at the shifting cloud and pressed a trigger for the first time in my life. I jolted at the whip of the gun and watched a bird explode in mid-air and tumble acrobatically. It flapped its last and disappeared beneath us towards the street.

The grey flock of birds sheered away without missing a beat. They took a high straight line away from the city, then began to repeat their circle in a new piece of sky near the wider blue of the lake.

'Well done! You killed it. Well done!'

Amadori laughed long as if no one had ever really understood him. As if only he could see the world this way and no one had ever shared his vision. Then he grabbed back the gun like I had stolen it from him, placed it down by the low wall, straightened his shoulders and adjusted his suit jacket.

He looked off across the city again. 'So, the drop dead date is this Friday at five,' he said, as if I'd distracted him and he had to remember the reason for the meeting, 'and a body has been found floating in the lake.'

He looked at me as if I knew all about it. As if I might have answers.

'And a coin commemorating a hundred years of Amadori business was in the dead man's mouth.' He chewed up his doll's face as if he could taste the metal. 'He was one of yours, Mr Seymour. A simple delivery guy.'

My blank expression said I had nothing to add.

He sighed and gestured towards the wide, empty roof of the Amadori headquarters. 'This is my new office. I've moved out before the drop dead date.' He looked hurt. 'There is nowhere else I can talk. There is nothing I should hear. The lawyers from both sides have been swarming the building for weeks.' He pouted like a sulking boy. 'I'm told I am only the owner.'

I nodded this time. I'd shifted a long way down from my corporate past but I knew that a drop dead date meant serious consequences to a company if a major deal wasn't signed on time. I also knew that the heightened emotions of an owner during a sale could easily smudge the paperwork. The final closing of a deal was often best left to the professionals.

This was my moment to escape from the unhinged man.

'And I am so glad we will be working together this week,' said Amadori with a sudden grin.

I breathed. A long, low breath. It was clear that there had been a serious mistake. I had been confused with someone else. Keep it polite, I thought, very polite and then leave. Fast.

'Mr Amadori,' I said quietly. 'I was called here for a collection.'

'Yes, falsely,' he said. 'Sorry.' His lips tightened. 'But instead, we have an agreement.' It seemed to have been discussed and settled. 'I'm buying you until Friday. Ten thousand Swiss.'

He provided a prompt hand for me to shake. I didn't take it. I looked backwards and forwards between his white teeth, the grey line on his forehead and his small hand reaching out to me. I counted to ten.

Amadori sighed with impatience, as if he was so tired of managing people, then withdrew a thin white envelope from his pocket, opened it and counted out ten crisp, violet thousand franc notes. I had never seen the pride of Switzerland's currency in a man's hand. It was more money than I'd seen for a long time. It was enough for survival in this shiny, over-priced city. But it was a mistake. I had no idea why I was here, or if I should have been someone else. I had my rules and, until Friday, I still had David to protect. A small shake of my head told Amadori that whatever had been planned, whatever confusion I had stepped inside, was not going to happen.

Amadori dropped his empty hand and looked off again across the city.

'You are Mr Seymour? Mr Bill Seymour?'

It was a rule that I never spoke my new name, but somehow he knew it.

'Can I ask you a personal question, Mr Seymour?'

It was always best to say nothing. Another of my reinvention rules.

'Mr Seymour, have you ever suffered from high self-esteem?'

I said nothing. The rules were the rules.

'Well?' he pressed. 'Have you?'

Sometimes rules had to be bent. 'I don't believe I have, Mr Amadori,' I said.

'Victor. Victor, please!' he said, as if I'd refused to be his best friend.

'I don't believe I suffer from high self-esteem, Victor,' I said.

Amadori gazed off into the horizon as if it would add meaning to what he was about to say. 'I suffer from it all the time,' he said and squeezed his eyes together in an attempt to make them look pained. 'You must excuse me. I do forget that people have their own important lives.'

There was only one way out left. The word no wasn't used with men like this, but it was often the only language they understood.

'Mr Amadori. There has been a mistake. I run a delivery business. If you have something for me to collect?'

Victor Amadori looked me up and down and I felt like something he had bought and wasn't going to return. Even if what he saw in front of him was disappointing.

'There's no error, Mr Seymour. I've made a decision. You won't pedal away from my offer.' He took a step and moved very close to me and our bodies touched as he inserted the envelope into the back pocket of my cycling shirt. 'Treat this delivery as a deposit, Mr Seymour,' he whispered.

I stared out across the low-rise old city. The jumble of red roofs and square buildings looked like a row of dice ready to be rolled. I knew there was trouble here. Corporate trouble. Rule-breaking trouble. Amadori couldn't possibly know how much I needed this money to survive.

'I try to make an honest living, Mr Amadori,' I said. Then I looked off beyond him at where dark thunderheads were starting to build across the Alps. A low, distant rumble suggested a different answer to the hot day.

'But I'll think about it.'

And there it was again. The old problem. Seeping back in as I walked back to the service lift. Why hadn't I walked away? Why hadn't I handed the money back? I had my own Drop Dead Date. I had gestated my new identity in this foreign city for almost nine months. Friday was the day that I would complete my rebirth as Bill Seymour.

But I knew the answer.

Too much David, and not enough Bill.

CHAPTER TWO

The two large-muscled women approach the body. One holds a ball of rough string and a reel of black thread. The other a handful of thick needles, a bicycle pump and some brown resin plugs. They place the equipment on a small table. They raise the man's body carefully from the trolley, unwind the white sheet he is wrapped in and lower him back naked.

The place where my bullet entered his chest is a rough black pucker now, not the brown shredded hole it was before. One of the women takes a small resin plug, checks it for size between two fingers and pushes it into the wound. They roll his body over and look at the rise of flesh where the bullet reached the back of his chest but didn't find its way out. The women run their fingers over it as if they are curious.

One quickly divides the man's buttocks and the other slides a plug into him with a firm thumb. They turn him back over and move towards his head. One of them loads a needle with the black thread as the other retrieves a coin from a pocket, opens the man's mouth with her fingers and places it inside. The one with the needle checks the thread against the room's single light bulb before pushing it hard and sudden through the man's lower lip. She forces it to emerge above his top lip and begins her work. The man's mouth is pulled backwards and forwards as if he's making a silent protest. His chin is painted red by the time the thread's end is knotted and cut. His lips are finally sewn up and smaller resin plugs are squeezed into his ears and nose.

One of the women attaches a hypodermic needle to the end of a black bicycle pump as the other stretches a small area of the man's belly skin flat with her fingers. She pierces the skin with the needle and pumps hard into the man until his stomach is extended and full of air. Then the women stop and stand back from the body. They put their heads to one side and listen. There is no sound.

Now they lift, turn and manoeuvre the body between them and circle him with the rough string. They bind him tight until his arms are pressed like fillets against his sides; his legs are a divided trunk and his useless sex is squashed flat against his stomach.

I sit and nod my approval.

This one should float.

CHAPTER THREE

I'd worked my hands into the stickiness of my cycle gloves, wrapped my dark glasses around my head and tightened my helmet by the time the lift had reached the ground floor. I wanted to get on my bike and away.

I needed to interrogate David. I had money. A lot of money. Someone else's money. I needed to decide what to do with it.

Perhaps the bike would sort me out.

When I escaped from London to Geneva, nine months before, I didn't know about bikes, but I soon decided they were the perfect disguise for the reinvented. Difficult to trace. Impossible to follow in a city. Easy to replace if they were stolen. I had changed bikes regularly to stay below the radar, and the latest was my fourth. Dirty orange frame, black plastic saddle and scruffy white drops. Probably forty years old, and looking its age, but still working. Like me. I'd bought it on the Rue des Grottes near the needle exchange. Two hundred in cash made for a quick buy.

Easy. Invisible.

I stepped out of Amadori's headquarters and stopped.

A police car was parked by my locked bike and standing next to it was a very large, middle-aged woman dressed in an operatic curtain of black. She was partnered by a small, stocky, uniformed Geneva policeman. He was holding a dead pigeon. He was armed. Both were looking at the bike and nodding in agreement.

Shit.

It was too late to change course. I was the only civilian on the street and the only person dressed for a bike. I had no identification. Follow the rules, I told myself. I walked towards the bike as the woman angled her width towards me and placed her hands on her hips.

'*Bonsoir!*' I tried with false cheer. A tourist trying out a few local words. I moved to the bike and bent down to undo the heavy, u-shaped lock.

'Good evening, *monsieur*,' the woman replied, noting my accent in an instant.

She and the uniform both took a well-practised step towards me.

'We have been looking at this bike, *monsieur*,' she said in slow, deliberate English, scanning me up and down.

'Is it yours? The bike. Is it yours?'

'Yes, this is my bike.' I stood up and gripped the lock in front of my crotch like a weapon.

I had avoided contact with the authorities for almost nine months. Now this.

The uniformed policeman moved closer to the bike. He stroked the metal frame with one hand and held the dead pigeon away from him with the other.

'*C'est un Cilo*,' he said, addressing the bike rather than me.

'*Seelo?*' I said. 'I'm sorry. *Desolé. Je ne parle pas francais.*'

I'd learned quickly that murdering a language could speed an escape. Not today.

'*C'est un Cilo, monsieur. Un Cilo.*' The uniform shook his head with disbelief.

'He says it's a *Cilo*,' said the large woman with the forced patience of a teacher.

'C-I-L-O. *Cilo.*' She was clearly the senior of the two. 'A *Cilo*. Made in Switzerland. Designed just for the police. I am the Chief of Police.'

'*C'ést un miracle*,' said the uniform, patting the seat like an old friend.

'He says the bike "it is a miracle",' repeated the Chief of Police. 'He has not seen a *Cilo* for many years. He used to ride one. Just like this. When he had *commencé*. The police have not used these bikes for many years.' Her face folded into a look of regret. 'Now they are *fabriqué* in Taiwan.'

'*Ah, trés bien.* Good,' I said, taking hold of the bike and making a show of starting to move away.

'Stop,' she said, spreading her arms and blocking my exit.

I counted to ten.

'You look concerned,' she said. 'Has something upset you?'

I didn't answer. She waited for a few seconds then gave up and smiled at me with genuine warmth.

'Well, we would like to thank you,' she said. 'For showing us this very special bicycle.'

'*Oui. Merci, monsieur*,' said the uniform, shaking his head and putting a finger to an eye to stop a tear forming. '*Merci, encore.*'

'And now we wish you a *bonne soirée, monsieur*.'

She lowered her arms and took a gracious step back to allow me to move forwards with the bike. I pushed it fast across the little square, looking back once to see the policeman drop the dead pigeon into a bin, brush his hands together then run a few steps to catch up with the large woman. He reached her and held open the door of the Amadori building with a small flourish as she swept inside.

Shit.

I lifted onto the bike and strained my legs against the pedals with an urgency I hadn't felt since I had arrived. I careered away from the pedestrian area down past the luxury fronts of the shopping district, and in less than a minute I was crossing the Mont Blanc bridge and pushing hard across the Rhone. I wove through three lines of Sunday tourist traffic and jumped lanes before skipping onto the pavement to avoid the lights at the end of the bridge. The lake parade of starred hotels and parked up limousines blurred behind me as I swung up into the quieter, narrow streets of Le Pâquis. I rolled to the kerb by my basement office, stopped the bike badly with heavy brakes and breathed out.

The stiff little envelope of money was pressing uncomfortably into my back.

My only visibility in this new city was the small sign that I'd glued that morning to the dirty yellow wall by the basement stairs – *Secure By Hand.* It was an early celebration of nine months in this new country, and of what I had told myself was my second coming. I had felt brave putting up the sign after months living inside the control experiment that I called Bill Seymour.

I should have known that brave was better left behind.

Yes, I had found it difficult at first, working for a world that I'd once decided to hate. But I wasn't alone in that. I still needed money to live. How many of us are there? Seven billion? But at least now I was the boss. For the first time in my life I could define the daylight hours, be the guiding sun, the rule book, the one that could make or break. That was new, after decades of being a loyal cog in a global corporate fleet.

Yes, it had taken me years to find the problem in the engine room, but it hadn't taken me long to tell the truth. I had no idea that when I raised the alarm how far I would sink with the ship. The threats to my whistle-blower's life had made me leave London in a silent, terrified rush.

Less than a year later, this new city supported my knocked-up existence as Bill Seymour. My continuity. Job by job. Now I took people's money, probably not theirs, for delivering documents across the city by bike. This was a country that still respected the value of discretion, wet ink and personal delivery. The work was as perfectly analogue as I needed Bill to be. And to the outside world I was just another small business in another country. One of the invisible majority. Swimming like suckerfish along the scaly corporate back of the world. Trying not to get eaten in the process. I had scraped together a working life with a handful of bikes and a couple of part-time riders, Trip and Sven. Each of us, in our own way, meeting the job requirements of being damaged goods.

Odd, I often thought, given what we were carrying.

It was the city itself that had made my meagre cash-in-hand business possible. Untraceable document deliveries were still in high demand in Geneva because the company headquarters of the world were here. The sainted, tainted peace-making institutions. The fattest private banks. The richest commodity traders and the dirtiest money. European old, Russian new, China on its way and the Middle East, a constant dark flow.

They all needed a little paid help to keep their version of the world moving forwards.

Stumbling down the steps with the bike, I fumbled with the keys and entered my small basement office thinking hard about how the dead body of a courier could end up in a lake. That body could have been mine.

I removed the envelope from my shirt and counted out the thousand franc notes. I counted it out again and balanced in my hand. I raised it to my face and smelled it. I would have whistled if I hadn't learned how dangerous whistling could be. I counted to ten then unlocked a drawer and retrieved the large, almost empty, battered petty cash box. I slipped the envelope sensibly beneath a handful of letters and locked it. Then I paused, unlocked the box, retrieved the envelope, counted the money again and slipped one of the notes carefully into my cycle sock.

It was against the rules but I made an instant decision and put the envelope into the back pocket of my shirt.

I double-checked everything in the office. The window locks, the filing cabinet, the metal drawers in the desk. I pulled hard on each to test them, then turned off the office light and silenced the old air conditioning. I locked the door, pushed hard against it with my shoulder and walked up the stairs. I stopped to stare at my company name on the wall, then retrieved a small bike tool from my pocket, levered off the plaque and slid it into my shirt pocket.

I pushed the bike slowly up the one-way street towards my rented rooms, a few streets away, located above the Café du Môle. Until now I had felt invisible, buried among the honest and dishonest immigrants who populated the stolid apartment blocks of the Pâquis, the red light district below the station. Once a simple pasture that fed Calvin's walled city and its protestant work ethic, there was no grass here now. Only some heavy shutters rolled down to create a day's shade before the residents spread out across the morning into the opposite sides of the city. Every day they polished the floors and windows of vast lobbies, clipped the lawns and smoothed the paths for the influencers of the world, then returned, weary and stoic, to eat their home food at the end of the day.

But unlike the rest of this city, no one in the Pâquis cared about managing their reputation. And that suited me. Old men drank cans of beer in the street and spat on the pavement without a thought. Small groups of lads in sports caps hung around doorways using their phones to direct buyers towards them. A choir practised for Jesus in a courtyard. Sex workers on the Rue Sismondi sung a quiet *'Bonjour Chérie'* to any man who looked like he had the money and the balls. Only a few residents bothered to look up at the disinterested crawl of a police car. We all knew the area for what it was. Eritrean, Kurdistani, Greek, Italian, Indian, Chinese, Portuguese, Korean; the cafés and corner shops of a hundred nationalities dealing out dinner across the grid of the best and worst district in town.

Uniting nations? Possibly.

I crossed the road towards the Café du Môle, nodding towards an ageing prostitute who had been as permanent as street furniture since I'd arrived. She had purple hair, a leather-tied bodice and ripped fishnets that captured her small, triangular legs. She smiled at me with recognition and few remaining teeth.

I took the thousand-franc note out of my sock and handed it to her.

'For Marie,' I said, walking past her and not looking back.

I opened the side door by the café and left the street. It was cooler in the dark staircase, almost cold, and I shivered as I walked the four floors up knowing that these old stones and pipes would never smell like home. I arrived at my worn '*Bienvenue*' doormat and followed the rules. I let my heart slow, dropped my breathing and listened, as I had so many times. Then I unlocked the door in three places, entered the narrow hall, stripped off my shirt and hung it on the back of the door. I moved silently around the flat, checked the bedroom and the kitchen and turned on a lamp. I finally sat down on the old brown sofa and kicked off my trainers. I placed my tired feet on top of the suitcase that, after nine months, still sat in the middle of the room unpacked.

The money would allow Bill Seymour to survive, but I had broken the rules.

Five days, and I would have to run again.

Mark Wightman is an Edinburgh native who grew up in South East Asia. After what seemed like a lifetime working in information technology, he took time out to study creative writing. He won the Pitch Perfect competition at Bloody Scotland 2017 with *Waking the Tiger*, his debut novel.

mark.wightman@gmail.com

Waking the Tiger

CHAPTER ONE
30th December 1938

The *Batavian Princess* swayed in the ebbing tide and the hawsers, thick as a man's arm, that held her fast to the Tanjong Pagar dock creaked in protest. Abu Bakar smiled to himself. He loved these boats; he sensed their spirits. This one protested at the indignity of being forcibly restrained. 'Hurry,' she seemed to say, 'this place is not for me. I should be out there, at sea, not tied to this godforsaken piece of land.'

The passengers, Europeans coming from up-country to Singapore for the New Year's Eve celebrations, had disembarked. A few might return to their cabins after their evening's entertainment, but for now a skeleton crew and the tally clerk and his band of Chinese coolies had the ship to themselves.

One by one, Abu Bakar checked the boxes of cargo that the coolies had dragged up from the ship's hold against the manifest and made sure they carried the correct box off to the correct truck to begin the next part of its journey.

He peered at the identifying marks scorched into a wooden tea chest, his eyes struggling to make out the characters. Either the shipping companies were getting more careless or his eyes were failing him, just as Noor, his wife, had suggested that morning when she had caught him holding his newspaper at arm's length and squinting at the news. She had chided him for not visiting Mr Foong, the optician on Bencoolen Street who provided, so her sister assured her, extremely reasonably priced spectacles. Abu Bakar had dismissed her ministrations with a sly insult concerning her sister's lack of judgement and a firm assertion that there were much better things on which they could spend their hard-earned money than overpriced spectacles. But perhaps she had a point, after all.

He resumed his checking and when he had accounted for the final piece, he signalled to the foreman for the coolies to begin moving the cargo off the ship. Two by two, the coolies shuffled up the gangplank. They looped canvas harnesses first around stout bamboo poles and then under the tea chests. Abu Bakar watched as their faces contorted with the strain of raising the poles onto their bony shoulders. He felt a pang of sorrow for them. They earned so little, and what remained after they paid those to whom they were indentured would doubtless be spent on opium to dull the few waking hours until it was time to work again. Or on the cheap whores of Malay Street or Smith Street where they would seek brief solace with women who were as much slaves as themselves. He gave each of the coolies a small smile of encouragement as they staggered past, but all he got in return were blank looks. It was as though their souls had been wiped from their bodies.

When the last of the chests had been removed, Abu Bakar climbed the metal staircase to the bridge above where he reported to the ship's first officer that all the cargo was accounted for and had been sent on its way. He handed the bill of lading to the young European who checked the time on a gold wristwatch and signed the manifest before dismissing the clerk with a curt nod.

Abu Bakar left the cabin and stretched. The wailing cry of the *adhan* tumbled over the roofs of the godowns that lined the river: *'There is no god but God; Muhammad is the messenger of God.'*

What was it with these young men and their wristwatches? They all seemed to want one. He remembered, earlier that day, watching two of the junior officers compare their new purchases, pleased with themselves for following the latest fashion. Abu Bakar smiled at the recollection of this folly; he had no need of a wristwatch; the position of the sun and the call of the *muezzin* were all he needed to know the time had come for him to return home to his wife and her sister and her spectacles.

He descended the metal gangway to the heat and noise of the dockyard below, and from his shirt pocket he pulled a packet of *kretek*, the pungent Indonesian spiced cigarettes the policeman, Betancourt, gave him in return for the occasional snippets of information he picked up around the wharves. Noor complained of the smell of cloves and wouldn't let him smoke them in the house, so he allowed himself one each day, on his way home. He struck a match and let it flare before cupping his hands around the flame.

As he dipped his head to light the tobacco, a movement in the shadow of a large jacaranda tree near the gate to the dockyard caught his eye. He peered into the shade. There it was again. He waited for his eyes to focus and started at the sight of a huge brown rat, gnawing at the edges of a weather-beaten green tarpaulin. The rat, sensing it was being watched, stopped eating and took refuge behind the tree. It sniffed the air, its long whiskers twitching. Abu Bakar kept his gaze fixed on the whiskers, which were all he could now see of the animal. He scrabbled around on the ground for something heavy and found a piece of broken brick. Mustering his strength, he fired the brick in the direction of the whiskers. The rodent dodged the missile with ease and gave Abu Bakar an indignant stare before scurrying off towards the sanctuary of a pile of abandoned tyres.

Rats were a common enough sight around the godowns where the rice was stored, but it was rare to see them here on the open ground and Abu Bakar wondered what the animal had found to tempt it out like this. As he approached the mound, his foot stuck to the hot tarmacadam. He had trodden in a rivulet of semi-congealed blood. Stepping back, he wiped his sandal on a clump of sea grass that sprouted up through a crack in the tar before he peered again at the tarpaulin, puzzled. Occasionally, trucks rumbling into the yard to deliver or pick up cargo would hit a cat that failed to get out of the way quickly enough. He was forever imploring the drivers to slow down, but the shipping agents paid the drivers by the load and the quicker they got in, loaded up, and away, the quicker they could be back for their next load. Maybe someone had seen a dead cat and covered it up. But this was much too big for a cat. A dog, perhaps? No. A pig? But who would kill a pig here, in the middle of the dockyard, and leave it to bleed?

Gingerly, he lifted the edge of the tarpaulin and peered underneath. Momentarily confused, he saw a shoe – a bright green woman's shoe. Silk, he wondered? Yes, rough silk, studded with knots and nubs. The same material as the *sarong kebaya* his wife wore on the most special occasions. Still confused, he stood and drew back the rest of the cover. He rocked backwards, appalled to see the body of a young woman. She wore a dress which matched the shoe, and a green jewelled necklace and earrings that glinted as they caught the afternoon sun. The dress was a tight-fitting *cheongsam*-style sheath, which would have hugged her figure had the front of it not been ripped open and pulled apart to leave her naked and exposed from the waist down. She lay on her back, arms folded across her chest, as though prepared for burial. Bloody marks ran from the black triangle between her legs to the tops of her stockings, and the blood had dried brown, throwing the paleness of her skin into stark relief. The fingertips of one of her hands were missing, chewed off, Abu Bakar presumed, by the giant rat. Her head twisted away at an unnatural angle, towards the trunk of the tree, as if she were staring intently at the bark, and Abu Bakar had to walk round to the other side to see her face. A snail had left a shiny trail across the ashen skin from her eye to her throat, where it had halted at the edge of a ragged, gaping hole. Abu Bakar had seen plenty of goats being slaughtered in his time, but those had been swift, clean cuts. Whoever killed this woman had nearly decapitated her.

He felt the acid bile rise in his throat and sobbed a hurried, incoherent blessing wishing the woman safe passage to heaven, before swinging round and retching until nothing remained inside him.

The air in the small office occupied by Sub-Inspector Maximo Betancourt of the Marine Police was as still as a dead cat in a gutter. He reached behind him to open the shutters in a futile attempt to let a breeze into the room. The unique smell of the Singapore River – a mixture of diesel oil, human detritus, and the sea, which Betancourt called 'the aroma of commerce' – drifted in through the rattan blinds.

He fanned himself idly with a copy of the day's *Straits Tribune*. A mosquito circled, too small for him to see but audible over the background noise of the activity on the river. Betancourt squinted through the late afternoon light, rolled up the newspaper, and took aim.

'Missed, damn it,' he said out loud to the empty room and opened the newspaper again. He leafed lackadaisically through the pages until a passage from a column in the Foreign News section caught his eye.

Another Siam Opium Seizure
CID officers and men raided a godown in Bangkok last week and seized over fifty tahils of prepared opium, together with various paraphernalia used for boiling the drug. The gang fled the premises, and no arrests were made.

He gave an indignant snort. Fifty *tahils*? Not even five pounds. Why did they bother? The Siamese police boasted about taking fifty *tahils,* yet there were thousands of *tahils* making their way into the opium houses of Singapore every week. The lucrative trade in opium, so long the prime source of revenue for the European mercantile houses whose godowns lined the river, had been illegal these past four years. Not that the change in the law had made an iota of difference to Betancourt and his small band of customs officers. If anything, the quantities of the drug entering the colony had increased, and he despaired of ever being able to stem the tide.

He continued to turn the pages of the newspaper until he reached the arrivals and departures section, and his eyes ran down the list of ships which had recently entered or were due to leave Singapore waters. There would be little activity in the port until the New Year's festivities were over – the *tuans* and their *mems* didn't like to sail with a hangover – an observation that did nothing for his insouciance. He was scribbling the names of ships he would need to check when the discordant jangle of the telephone echoed through the room. He scowled at the receiver before lifting the handset.

'Marine Branch.' He sat up, all attention, and listened for a moment before picking up a pen. He wrote quickly in the margin of the newspaper.

'When? Are you sure?' He put down the pen and leaned back in his chair.

'But why Marine?' He was silent for a while, listening intently. 'I see. Yes. Of course. I'll leave immediately.' There was another pause as he received his final instructions, and he swore softly under his breath before replying. 'Must I? Very well, I'll meet him at the dockyard.'

CHAPTER THREE

A broad plaza separated the Government Buildings on Empress Place from the Singapore River, which glided past on its way to emptying out into the Singapore Straits. In the centre of the plaza stood Sir Stamford Raffles, arms crossed, one leg in front of the other, haughtily surveying his subjects as they scuttled about their business of administering to the colony he had established over a hundred years ago. Betancourt stooped to touch the base of the statue. He had forgotten why he'd started doing this, but his superstitious nature assured him that ill luck was likely to befall him if he ever stopped.

He crossed the river at Cavenagh Bridge, hurrying towards Collyer Quay and the docks beyond. As he did so, a large, grey-backed gull bobbed past, navigating the river atop an upturned orange crate. The bird cocked its head at him and held his gaze with its black eyes as if enquiring what all the rush was about. It seemed oblivious to the buzz of the bumboats which criss-crossed the river like so many water beetles. The boat drivers cursed and shouted at one another as they jockeyed for position, each fighting his neighbour for the next commission to ferry a load of rice or rubber or palm oil from the godowns along the riverfront to one of the countless boats lying anchored in the Straits offshore.

Two years of rubber-stamping documentation, counting boxes of cargo, and trapping smugglers of small amounts of minor contraband had taken their toll on Betancourt and lately he had lapsed into a semi-permanent ennui. The opportunity of doing what he considered real police work again excited him and he moved with a purpose long missing.

A call from Anthony Beecham, the Assistant Commissioner, was both rare and unexpected. A call instructing Betancourt to investigate a dead body as a matter of the utmost urgency was unheard of these days. When he asked why the Detective Branch hadn't assigned one of their own men to the case, Beecham reminded him, with an uncharacteristic mixture of curtness and equivocality, that the woman – 'probably just some doxy who pushed her luck too far' – had been found within the confines of the Port of Singapore and, per the Maritime and Port Authority Act, jurisdiction lay with the Marine Police.

As he passed through the gates of the dockyard, he remembered, ominously, Beecham had also told him he was to be provided with assistance.

At the far end of the dock a white-painted ship bearing the legend *Campbell & Rutherford* on its single funnel lay bound to the harbour wall.

About fifty yards from the ship's gangway a small group of uniformed Europeans stood huddled together, speaking to each other in low voices. A few yards away an older Malay man stood on his own, head bowed. Betancourt knew the man to be a friendly, gregarious sort. He wouldn't stand away from the group of sailors by choice; it was obvious he was just not welcome.

Over by the dockyard wall, the branches of a jacaranda tree in glorious full bloom provided cover for a group of coolies who had gathered in the shade of its purple canopy, jostling and straining to catch a glimpse of the dead woman.

A young policeman wearing the khaki of the main force and brandishing a notebook and pencil scurried over to introduce himself. Betancourt pre-empted him with a raised hand.

'Don't tell me. Sergeant Quek.'

The sergeant's eyes widened. 'How did you know?'

The last thing Betancourt needed or wanted was a greenhorn tagging along, getting in the way, but Beecham had been insistent.

'Because I'm a detective.' He sighed. 'Firstly, the AC said I was to expect you, and secondly, your name is on your badge.' He tapped the younger man's chest. 'Now watch, listen, and learn. This is how it's going to work. I'll ask the questions and you'll write everything down. *Everything*. Got it?'

'Yes, Inspector.' Quek nodded several times, all the time scribbling away furiously in his notebook.

Betancourt laid a hand on the frenetic pencil. 'You don't have to write down everything I say. Save it for the witnesses.'

'Yes, Inspector,' Quek repeated, copying down what Betancourt had just said.

Betancourt shook his head. 'And you don't have to keep calling me Inspector, either. Boss is fine.'

'Yes, Insp—, yes, boss.'

'Good. Now follow me, and we'll try to find out what happened here.'

He pushed his way through the gawking rabble, barking instructions in Malay and rudimentary Hokkien. When he reached the front, he greeted the police photographer, a man named Phun, with whom he had worked when he was still *persona grata* at the Detective Branch in Hill Street.

'How long till you'll have the photographs developed?'

The man shrugged. 'Day after tomorrow?'

'I want them on my desk tomorrow morning. No later than midday.'

'Very busy, *lah*. I try.'

'Tomorrow morning,' Betancourt repeated. 'Understood?'

Phun nodded sullenly and continued with his intimate photo-study.

Dr Granville, the police doctor, a slight, dapper man, was bent over the body. There was even less breeze in the lee of the ship than there had been by the river. The dipping sun glinted off the man's bald head and Betancourt noticed it was beaded with tiny balls of perspiration. As if hearing his thoughts, Granville produced a bright red handkerchief from the pocket of his linen jacket, and with an exaggerated flourish, mopped away the moisture.

His lips moved soundlessly as he continued his survey and as Betancourt approached him he nodded to himself in apparent satisfaction, making a note in a small embossed leather notebook with a tiny silver pencil.

'Ah, Betancourt. How long has it been? A year?'

Betancourt shook the proffered hand. 'More like two. What's the verdict?'

Granville pointed to the wound on the woman's throat. 'It would have been quick. The cause of death, at least, looks cut and dried.'

Betancourt raised an eyebrow at the pun, and the doctor gave an apologetic shrug.

'Anything to identify her?'

Granville shook his head. 'Not yet. There's no sign of a purse and nothing engraved on the jewellery which might tell us who she was.'

'So, they took her purse, but left her jewellery?' He turned to Quek. 'You're getting all this, aren't you?' Quek nodded without looking up from his note-taking.

'How long has she been dead?'

The doctor crouched and pointed to what looked like light bruising on the woman's side, where the skin touched the tarmac. 'Livor mortis has begun but discolouration is still relatively faint. Based on that, my guess would be more than six hours, but less than twenty-four. I'll know better when I've taken her back to The Crypt and done the post-mortem.'

Betancourt gave an involuntary shudder. The mere thought of the cavernous subterranean room below the river on Clarke Quay, which served as the police mortuary, made him nervous. He slackened his collar.

'But the Malay fellow,' the doctor continued, pointing across the yard to where Abu Bakar stood, 'said he stepped in the blood and it was still tacky. In this heat that would suggest less than an hour, two at most. It's odd.'

Betancourt turned to Quek again, only to find him giving a pre-emptive thumbs-up. 'Got it, boss.'

Something had struck Betancourt about the way the doctor had described the woman's death. 'You said *at least*. "The cause of death, *at least,* looks cut and dried." What did you mean?'

'Well, that's the other odd thing. Look at the blood – it's wrong.'

Betancourt stared. At first, he could see nothing out of the ordinary. Then he realised what Granville had seen and he had missed.

'Her throat...'

'Exactly. There's a trail flowing away from the body.' The doctor indicated the stream Abu Bakar had stepped in earlier, now dry and baked a burnt umber by the sun. 'And there are marks on the body.' He pointed to the daubs on the woman's legs. 'But there doesn't appear to be anything emanating from the wound itself.'

Betancourt nodded to himself, taking in the doctor's points.

'You're thinking someone killed her elsewhere and then moved her here? But then where would the fresh blood have come from?'

'I'm not thinking anything yet. But like I said, it's odd.'

Betancourt circled the body, looking for anything that might shed light on what had happened to her, but there was nothing more. He would just have to wait for the post-mortem.

As he turned back towards the jacaranda tree, a momentary flash of reflected sunlight glinted off something on the ground and dazzled him. He raised an arm and walked towards where he thought the light had come from. He poked at the dockyard detritus with his foot; an empty Spam can, already rusting in the salt air; a chipped and scuffed beer bottle; the remains of a hastily-taken meal – chicken rice in banana leaf by the looks of it; a discarded playing card. Nothing shiny enough to reflect light like that.

He became aware again of the crowd still packed around the tree, ogling the dead woman. 'Get her covered up and out of here, Doctor.'

He turned to the gang of coolies. 'Back up!' he shouted, and waved his arms, shooing them away in the direction of the pier.

Down here, there were always those who would rather not attract any undue attention from the authorities and several of the coolies had peeled off from the main group and were making their way back into the bowels of the docks, casting wary eyes over their shoulders. Betancourt sent Quek off in pursuit.

'When you've rounded them up and brought them back, meet me over there,' he said, pointing to the small group huddled near the ship.

As Betancourt approached, a sparse, nervous-looking man broke away from his colleagues and hurried forwards, half walking, half running. The legs which protruded from his starched white shorts were like two bowed sticks, thin and brown and knobbly. He reminded Betancourt of the little jockeys at the racecourse at Bukit Timah. The man introduced himself as Newsom, the captain of the *Batavian Princess.* He wrung his hands repeatedly when he spoke, as though trying to expunge a stain.

'It's a bad business, Inspector, a terrible business. The passengers will be returning soon to dress for dinner and I can't have them seeing policemen and doctors and a... a...'

Betancourt let him struggle for a few seconds before interrupting. 'A dead woman?'

'Quite. Any chance of getting all this cleared up quickly?' His face screwed up in distaste at the word *this*, and he waved a hand towards the tarpaulin, now roped off from the crowd of onlookers.

Betancourt gave a non-committal shrug.

The captain led the policemen over to the huddled group and introduced two younger men, also dressed in the white of the shipping line. 'This is Mr Harvey, my first officer. He was on watch when the... when it was found. And this is Jenkins, our deck cadet.'

Betancourt waited for the captain to introduce the elderly Malay standing behind the main group.

Newsom caught the direction of his gaze. 'Oh, that's just Bakar, the tally clerk. He made the discovery and alerted Harvey here. There's no need to involve him. Harvey will give you all the details.'

Betancourt ignored the captain's advice. He walked over and took the man's hand and greeted him in Malay. 'Good evening, *encik*. We'll need to ask you a few questions. We'll try not to detain you too long. Would you like to call your wife, to let her know you may be late?'

The old man thanked him. 'We don't have a telephone in our house, but my neighbour has one. I'll call him, and he'll let my wife know, so she doesn't worry.'

Betancourt shook Abu Bakar's hand again and returned to the ship's company.

'When did you berth?'

Newsom lifted his cap and ran a hand through his thinning sandy-coloured hair before answering. 'Around one o'clock. We were due in first thing, but there was a fire on board a palm oil lighter in the Straits off St John's Island. We had to sit offshore until they could tow her to safety and by that time we'd missed the tide.'

'And the passengers disembarked as soon as you arrived?'

'More or less. There were the usual formalities to complete. Your chaps checking papers and such like.'

'How many passengers did you have on board?'

'About twenty-four, give or take.'

'Give or take? You're not sure?'

The captain glanced at his first officer.

'That's about right, isn't it?'

Harvey nodded. 'Yes, that sounds about right.'

'I'll need to see the passenger manifest.'

Harvey took a step forward. 'Is that necessary? I mean, it's obvious the woman was just some tart who pushed her luck too far.'

The earlier conversation with Beecham echoed in Betancourt's mind: *Some doxy who pushed her luck too far.*

'Obvious, Mr Harvey? It's not at all obvious to me. Unless you know something you're not telling me.'

Newsom glared at his first officer, stifling any reply he might have been about to make. 'That's enough, Harvey.' Satisfied he had the situation back under his control, he instructed the third member of their party. 'Jenkins, fetch the passenger list.'

The deck cadet jogged away to find the documentation.

Betancourt noted the exchange between the two senior men, but continued as though nothing had happened. 'What time did the tally clerk alert you to what he'd discovered?'

Harvey appeared to have been mollified by the rebuke from Newsom, and when he replied his voice had lost a good deal of its earlier truculence. 'Around five. I remember he came up to the bridge, to let me know the unloading of the cargo was complete. I checked the time when I signed off the dispatch note. It can't have been more than a quarter of an hour after that the... the woman was found.'

Betancourt checked the time. It was past six. He had received the call from Beecham at around quarter past five, so that, at least, tied in.

'And I take it none of you heard or saw anything unusual today.'

The men shook their heads.

He turned back to Newsom. 'How many crew do you have?'

'Twelve in total. I've released the other men for shore leave. We keep a skeleton crew on board the ship when we're berthed. I was just about to head off myself when Harvey alerted me to what had happened.'

'A dozen crew members for twenty-four passengers? Isn't that rather a lot?'

'The crew have other duties. We're mainly a cargo ship.'

Betancourt nodded and gathered his thoughts.

'You mentioned earlier that passengers might return this evening. Is it normal for passengers to stay on board when the ship is in port?'

'It isn't common, but it isn't unknown. Some of the passengers are down for the New Year's celebration before returning to Swettenham when we sail on the fourth. As the company is paying, I suppose they thought they might save a bit of money by staying on board.'

'The company?'

Newsom's face registered surprise at the question.

'Campbell's. We're a Campbell and Rutherford ship and the passengers were mostly Campbell's men.'

'There were no women on the ship? These men didn't bring their wives with them?'

Newsom stole another quick glance in Harvey's direction and Betancourt caught the merest shake of a head.

'They're single men. Plantation managers, that sort of thing. No wives.'

The light was slipping away as the tropical night descended and Betancourt decided there was little more to gain. Taking the passenger manifest from the now-returned Jenkins, he thanked the captain and his men for their time and requested they contact him at the station on Empress Place if anything else came to mind.

With Quek in tow, he walked back towards the ship where he found Abu Bakar smoking, waiting patiently astride a bollard that years of chafing ropes had polished as smooth as glass. The old man's cigarette hissed and crackled as the rough mix of cloves and tobacco burned. Through plumes of scented smoke, he recounted his story, confirming that when he had finished unloading the cargo he had gone to find *Tuan* Harvey. He wasn't exactly sure of the time as he didn't wear a wristwatch himself, but he recalled *Tuan* Harvey had written five o'clock on the lading document. When he'd left the ship, the *muezzin* had been calling, and it was shortly afterwards he had discovered the body.

Betancourt thanked him, and said he would be in touch if there were any further questions.

Turning to Quek, he said: 'After you're finished with our friend here, you can start taking statements from that lot.' He nodded towards the group of coolies huddled under the jacaranda tree. 'Nobody will have seen anything, of course – nobody ever sees anything down here – but it's worth a try. I'll see you in the office tomorrow morning. Don't be late.'

Off to the west, towards Sumatra, sheets of lightning arced across the night sky in an electrical extravaganza. Betancourt shivered. He turned up the collar of his uniform as futile protection against the forces of nature and headed back towards the lights of the city.

Matt Willis has been lost in the Sahara, arrested in Iran, robbed by a Togolese witch doctor and attacked by a pack of Russian street dogs, but such incidents have never made the pages of the travel guides he has written. In his debut novel, *Caipirinha*, he explores the dark side of tourism.

matt.willis@yahoo.co.uk

Caipirinha

CHAPTER ONE

'A week? No chance, John. You've got a day.'

'Impossible.'

'I don't think I heard that. The line's bad. What did you say?'

A pause.

'John?'

'It can't be done in a day.'

Silence.

'How would you like Ulan Bator to be your next posting?'

'I'd rather you didn't threaten me, Malcolm.'

'Well, what would you prefer? Washington, Berlin... Paris? I can fix it, just get the deal signed by Thursday.'

'It's not that simple.'

'I haven't got time for this, John – it's just a bloody aircraft carrier, what's the hold-up?'

'There's a condition we can't possibly meet.'

'We've undercut the French, thrown in a state visit and God knows how many years of maintenance, what more do they want?'

'It's not the price, Malcolm.'

'Well what the hell is it?'

A pause.

'Is the line secure your end?'

'Of course.'

'OK. Remember the big tech deal I worked on last year?'

'Getting one of our lot started in Rio?'

'Yes.'

'What about it?'

'Did I ever mention the chickens?'

'Chickens? No, you didn't mention any chickens.'

'No, well I didn't put them in the report either. The Brazilian investors wanted ten live chickens. Didn't seem much to ask, so I agreed.'

'Where's this going, John?'

'They sacrificed the chickens to bless the deal, Malcolm. Spread the blood over the boardroom table, daubed it on our foreheads.'

Silence.

'Why didn't you tell me?'

'We decided to keep quiet about it. Seemed pretty harmless and the Brits were embarrassed – the CEO's suit was ruined.'

'But why?'

'*Umbanda* – Brazilian voodoo – the locals are hooked on it, had a shaman do the ritual.'

'Jesus.'

'That was a five million deal, Malcolm, the aircraft carrier's half a billion. We're in a different league now.'

'So?'

'So they've brought in an Amazonian shaman – one that does *Quimbanda*, much darker than *Umbanda*.'

'Meaning?'

'It's not chickens this time, Malcolm.'

'Well what the hell is it?'

'The Brazilians have been told to bring a foreigner to the signing ceremony and we're supposed to provide a local girl.'

'Jesus Christ! You mean human sacrifice?'

'I don't know, I can't say. I hope not.'

'What can you do?'

'If I had a week, I could visit a few contacts in São Paulo and Brasilia – see if we could use their influence – and I'd have time to fly out to the Amazon, speak to some tribal elders, maybe they'd rein the shaman in a bit.'

A pause.

'Intelligence says the French are flying in a better offer on Friday, John. We're fucked if you don't seal this tomorrow. I'm relying on you. And I mean it about Washington and Paris – you know we can make it happen.'

'And you mean it about Ulan Bator?'

Silence.

'Can you find what they want, John?'

'What?'

'A girl?'

'Are you mad? I'm the ambassador for God's sake! I can't go around procuring young women!'

'You're in Rio, John, how difficult can it be?'

'We're supposed to prevent trafficking, not engage in it!'

'Listen, I'm pressed for time, but think about this – we'll go along with it and have our people standing by to make sure no one gets hurt. How about that?'

'I'm not getting involved, Malcolm. Even if I wanted to, I couldn't

– everyone knows me here.'

'But you could help someone facilitate it, perhaps?'

'Who?'

'Haven't you got a First Secretary there?'

'You mean Simon? Simon Muthers? He only arrived yesterday – he barely knows his way to the office.'

'Does he speak the lingo?'

'Yes.'

'Good, well, that'll do. Tell him he'll be well looked after – big promotion by September, no question.'

'I don't know, Malcolm, this could get very messy.'

'Just keep everything verbal, John – no emails, no texts, no paper trail. Look, I've had the Saudi trade minister on hold for half an hour already – must dash – call me at the same time tomorrow with some news.'

'But Malcolm—'

The dialling tone silenced him.

John reached across the table to pause the recorder then slipped off his headphones, leant forward and stabbed at the limes in his cocktail with a straw.

'I recorded that this afternoon,' he said. 'You know who it was?'

Simon had removed his earphones and was coiling the cable around a finger.

'Malcolm Symonds?'

'Good, yes – International Trade Secretary. Powerful chap.'

Cool air wafted down from the overhead fan, the swish of its blades a backdrop to the mellow beats drifting from the bar. Simon shifted in his chair and examined his fingers. John took a sip of his cocktail, set it down on the table and looked across at him.

'What do you think?'

Simon ran his hand through his hair.

'I have... I had no idea things were done like this.'

'You have,' said John with a glance at his watch, 'a day to find us a local girl.'

CHAPTER TWO

'What the fuck are you staring at, Jase?'

A thong lost between the cheeks of a tanned arse that shook to the music's beat. He couldn't see the face, was waiting for her to turn.

'You're looking at that girl again, aren't you? That bloody whore!'

The words came like three sharp slaps, loud and hard.

'I'm not!'

He switched his focus to Marie, saw the hurt obscuring her pretty face and broke eye contact to stir his cocktail. They'd had three or four, strong and sickly sweet with a name he could never remember.

'It's our bloody honeymoon Jase, how could you?'

Tears glistened in her eyes while street lights fought the darkening sky and beachgoers, tiny in the distance, were heading home. Reaching across the table for her hand, he clasped it in both of his, stroked her slender fingers one by one down to each of their neat scarlet nails and met her eyes with a smile.

'Bastard,' she hissed and pulled free of his grasp.

'I was just thinking what a wonderful evening it was,' he murmured, 'and how gorgeous you're looking. It's perfect here.'

He leaned towards her and slid his thumb gently across the wetness beneath her eye, pushing a mascara smear from left to right. No reaction. He wiped the teary residue on his shorts, took a sip from his drink.

'Want to dance?'

'No.'

'Oh, come on Marie.'

He stood up, swayed, and moved around the table. The place was full and waiters in grubby white shirts were ferrying drinks from the bar. Laying his hands on her bare shoulders from behind, he ran a finger under her bikini strap and lowered his mouth to her ear.

'I've only got eyes for you.'

His head dipped and she quivered as his tongue traced a cool line up her neck. She flicked locks of sun-bleached hair from her face, studied him sidelong with bleary eyes.

'You're drunk. Get lost,' she said, pushing him away with a shove that caught the table and toppled the cocktails, spilling ice and limes on their camera.

'Careful!'

Jase snatched it up, shook it and dabbed at the lens with a napkin. A waiter came to right the empty glasses. The armpits of his shirt were damp, his dark eyes tired.

'You want more drinks?' he asked.

'My husband's had enough, we're going home,' Marie slurred.

'You want taxi?'

'No, it's a beautiful evening, we'll walk to the bus station,' said Jase.

'Too dangerous now so late, you want taxi?

'Late? It's not late.' Jase gestured vaguely at the drowning sun.

Marie slapped the table.

'I want a taxi. Get us a taxi.'

The waiter looked from one to the other, hesitated and withdrew.

Jase stood gazing at the beach then turned, held out the camera at arm's length on its gimbal and began filming himself.

'So, here we are at the end of day three in Rio.'

He pointed the camera out to sea where ragged patches of peach-coloured sky were turning grey.

'It took us forever to find this place.'

He panned roughly around the bar.

'It's not on TripAdvisor, so no tourists, just a bunch of locals hanging out, a decent beach and...'

He focused on a barman shaking a mixer.

'...cheap cocktails! Marie'll tell you how to get here.'

He turned the camera on her, but she hid her face and flicked her middle finger.

'I'll cut that,' he said and switched back to himself.

'Well, it was a tram and a bus from Copacabana, that much I remember...'

He paused.

'... and now...'

He arched an eyebrow.

'... we've got to get back somehow.'

He dumped the camera and flopped into a chair. The waiter appeared beside them.

'No taxi, but there will be minibus soon. You take it?'

'Great!'

Marie rose, collected her bag and pulled away from Jase when he reached for her hand, but took his arm when they neared the dance floor and steered him through the girls shaking their slick bodies. Outside, the pulsing rhythm of cicadas swallowed the fading beats from the bar and the heat thickened beneath tall palms. A couple stood waiting at the roadside.

'Minibus?' Jase asked and they nodded.

He slid his arms around Marie's waist from behind and rested his chin upon her head, felt her stiffen then relax and sink back into his embrace.

'Bastard,' she murmured.

CHAPTER THREE

'Don't move!'

It was John, behind him. Simon tensed and lifted his gaze from the frothy pool forming in the urinal. He stared straight ahead, focused on the shimmer of a light bulb reflected in the glossy tiles and steadied his voice when he spoke.

'What's going on?'

'Wait.'

John's outstretched fingers came slowly into view to the left of Simon's head and then his arm and body followed as he lunged forward and slapped his open hand against the wall.

'Got it!' he said, standing back and examining the black smudge on his palm. 'Little bastard.'

Simon shook himself and zipped up.

'Mosquito?'

'An Aedes mosquito, you can tell by the white markings. Lethal.'

They stepped over to the basins. Simon lathered soap on his hands and spun the tap to rinse them.

'You scared me,' he said, coughing out a nervous laugh.

'I probably saved your life.'

John washed off the residue in the sink next to him, dried his hands and adjusted his tie in the mirror.

'Are you wearing repellent?' he asked.

Simon opened his mouth to speak, but nothing came and John grabbed his arm, pulled it up to his nose and sniffed.

'You're not. Haven't you read the safety briefing for God's sake? Repellent on exposed skin at all times!'

'I read most of it,' Simon began, his mind slow from the cocktails, 'I thought they only came out between dusk and dawn.'

'Wrong. They're at it round the clock here – different times of day, different disease risks. Yellow fever, Zika, chikungunya, dengue fever – all deadly.'

John straightened up, took a plastic bottle from his pocket and handed it to Simon then stepped over to the urinal and unzipped his fly.

'Put some of that on – arms, neck and behind your ears.'

Simon squirted a fine mist of repellent over his skin and winced when the acrid scent stung his nostrils.

John checked his watch and spoke to the wall.

'I have to run, do you need a lift to the office?'

'No, I've got some calls to make... as we discussed.'

Stepping back, John zipped up and washed his hands again before replying.

'Good,' he said with a rare smile. 'This deal will do wonders for your career and...,' he held Simon's gaze for a moment and his left eye twitched a rapid wink, '... for mine too – the ministry's very generous to those that go above and beyond.'

He clapped him on the shoulder with a damp hand and walked away.

Simon stared at the wall and rubbed his fingers over the stubble forming on his chin. He waited long enough to be sure John had left before going out through the bar and into the heat of the indigo sky.

CHAPTER FOUR

Some cars passed, a truck, a few hawkers struggling home with handcarts piled high and then a minibus approached at speed, its passengers a dark mass of heads, limbs and bags glimpsed through the open sliding door. A kid barely into his teens hung from the side and yelled out destinations as the driver braked suddenly and swung the wheels towards them.

'Flamengo?' asked Jase.

A woman clutching a tiny baby clambered out, the couple that had been waiting got in.

'*Flamayngu?*' the kid queried.

'Yeah, Flamengo. Are you going?'

'*Flamayngu, sim!*'

The kid grinned and pointed inside.

'*Vamos!*'

Jase climbed in behind Marie and a woman stuffed a large bundle under her seat to make space for them by the window. They sat down and the minibus pulled away. Holding out the gimbal with the lens facing him, Jase opened his mouth to speak, but was thrown forward when the driver braked sharply and the camera hit the passenger in front. The man grunted and twisted in his seat to glare at him. His eyes were small in a large face and held more anger than Jase had expected.

'*Filho de puta!*' he snarled.

'Sorry, really sorry!'

The man muttered something to the driver beside him who looked round at Jase before turning back to the road where a woman, white in the headlights, was flagging them down. The kid hanging off the minibus yelled at her and she yelled back. They stopped, she climbed in and they carried on.

Holding the gimbal more securely this time and squinting in the dazzle of the camera light, he positioned himself and Marie in the viewing screen and picked out the ghostly features of faces in the gloom behind.

'Local transport,' he began, then threw out a hand to steady himself and Marie grabbed his arm as the minibus swung left and right around a bend.

'Local transport... these minibuses are cheap, but not always cheerful,' he said with a glance at the back of the man's head in front.

'Hey mister, what you filming?' came a young voice from behind.

Jase brought the boy into focus – a kid in a faded football top, teeth and eyes shining in the light.

'You filming me?'

'Yeah, you're in our vlog now.'

'Vlog? You're vloggers?

'Yeah.'

'YouTube?'

'Yeah.'

'Famous?'

Jase smiled at the boy and then the camera.

'Getting there,' he said.

'What vlog?' the boy asked.

'Travel Makers.'

'Really? It's good name. My sister is vlogger in Santa Marta.'

'Santa Marta?'

'Is our place in Rio, everybody knows. Is favela, you know favela?'

'I've heard of them.'

'Is poor town mister, everybody poor, everybody crazy!'

'Is your sister famous?'

'Yeah,' he said with obvious pride, 'all Santa Marta know her.'

Marie turned to the boy.

'What does your sister vlog about?' she asked.

'She is beautiful vlogger.'

Marie smiled. 'Do you mean beauty vlogger? Lipstick and make-up and stuff?' She waved a hand over her face.

'Yes! Beauty vlogger,' he nodded, 'everybody like her!'

The girl next to the boy nudged him and spoke rapidly in Portuguese.

'She ask if this your husband.'

The boy grinned and the girl giggled.

Marie glanced at the lens, then looked up at Jase.

'Yeah,' she said, and smiled with happy eyes.

He switched off the camera and they were lost to the darkness. She laid her head on his shoulder.

'Sorry for getting so cross, Jase.'

He pressed his mouth into her hair, she lifted her face to his and he kissed her, shifted his legs, glanced forward and froze. The angry man was watching them, his head a black silhouette against the windscreen and his eyes, gleaming faintly, held Jase's for a moment before turning away.

Jase hugged Marie closer, patted his pocket and relaxed when he felt the comforting shape of his phone. He tilted his head to rest it upon hers, she mumbled something and streetlights splashed them orange.

Waves hissed white in the gloom as Simon stood outside the bar, waiting for a gap in the traffic separating the city from the sand. A red light stemmed the flow and he crossed towards the beach where the graffitied hood of a phone booth shone orange beneath a street light. Ducking under it, he lifted the receiver to his ear, pushed a phone card into the slot and tapped in the number he'd memorised.

He looked over his shoulder as it rang, saw a couple in swimwear walking hand in hand and a dog leading a jogger panting in the dark heat. The ringing stopped.

'Your number?'

The voice was scrambled, a genderless jumble of tones.

Simon cleared his throat.

'Forty-three,' he said.

'Forty-three... What's the weather like?'

He cupped his hand around the mouthpiece and spoke in a forced whisper: 'Your guess is as good as mine.'

'Go ahead Forty-three.'

'It's happened,' he said.

'Please clarify.'

'What you suspected would happen has happened.'

'Forty-three. Clarify please.'

Simon sucked warm air and steadied himself against the inside of the hood.

'The deal you spoke about last time – Eighteen is under pressure. There'll be some kind of voodoo ceremony... and you were right – he expects me to procure a girl for it.'

'And a man?' the voice asked.

'Yes, but that's for the Brazilians to sort out.'

'No further details?'

'The deal has to be signed by Thursday.'

'Good.'

'And...'

'Yes?'

'It may be bigger than you thought.'

'Go on.'

'The International Trade Secretary is directly involved.'

'I see. Can you be sure about that?'

'I heard a recording of their conversation.'

'Very good.'

'What do you expect me to do?'

The line crackled.

'Do exactly as Eighteen expects.'

'You're not serious?'

A car horn sounded nearby, he glanced behind and saw the gleaming bonnet of a limousine pulling up to the pavement. Turning back, he hunched over the phone and spoke firmly into the mouthpiece.

'Are you telling me to go along with this... this madness?'

'Affirmative Forty-three. Collect all possible evidence and...'

The car horn peeped again.

'Simon!'

'Shit!' he slammed down the phone and spun round, the limo was just a few feet away and John was watching him from its open rear window.

'Is your mobile on the blink?'

'No, no, it's fine,' Simon managed, 'I just had some credit on my phone card to use up.'

'Well, you may as well come with me, now that I've found you.'

'Where to?'

'I'll tell you on the way.'

The rear door swung open and Simon hesitated, looked left and right, saw the couple embracing beneath a palm tree and watched as a bus trundled past with a single passenger on board.

'Get in!'

With a last glance behind at the black and white sea, he got in and shut the door. Fat palm trunks slipped by his window as they pulled away and the air con chilled his moist skin.

'How did you find me?'

'I saw you crossing the street, got the driver to double back.'

Simon turned and saw John's face shifting from dark to light as car headlights flashed past.

'Are you going to the office?' he asked.

'No.' John shook his head. 'I'm going to see someone, someone who can help us.'

CHAPTER SIX

Marie and Jase woke abruptly when a sudden swerve to the right flung them left, their arms flailing for handholds; the minibus had turned off the main road and was rumbling along a rough track. Jase rubbed his eyes, looked around and wiped the sweat from his neck.

'*O que esta acontecendo*?' a woman shouted angrily at the driver.

'What's going on, Jase?'

'I don't know. Something's wrong.'

He peered through the windscreen, saw the track in the headlights and nothing beyond. The minibus stopped and the driver cut the engine, leaned back and lit a cigarette, the creaking springs of his seat amplified by the sudden silence.

'*O que esta acontecendo?*' the woman repeated, quieter now.

The angry man turned to face them, his head barely visible in the gloom.

'*Todos sair,*' he said.

'*Porque?*' the woman asked.

'*Todos sair!*'

Nobody moved. The man got out and walked around to the sliding door. The passengers muttered anxiously.

'Jase! What the hell is going on?'

He turned to the boy behind him.

'What's happening?'

The fear in the boy's eyes was enough.

'Bad men.'

The boy took out his phone, swiped the screen and it lit up his face.

'*Filho de puta!*' roared the man from outside.

He yanked open the door, reached in and hauled the boy outside, snatched the phone from his hand and threw it into the darkness then pushed him to the ground and swung a kick at his belly. The boy squirmed, gasping for breath and the girl leapt out, crouched over him and held up her palm at the man.

'*Por favor, deizho em paz!*' she begged.

Marie squeezed Jase's arm.

'If he touches her, I swear I'll bloody kill him!'

Jase looked down and saw her clenching a metal nail file.

'Shit Marie! Put that away! Don't do anything stupid for God's sake.'

The boy was sobbing, hugging his knees to his chin.

'*Deizho em paz,*' the girl repeated, her thin arm and determined eyes forming a protective shield, '*Por favor.*'

The angry man pulled back his hand to strike her.

'Don't you dare!' Marie screamed and thrust herself forward, scrambling over Jase's legs to get out, but he shoved her back, held her there and she struggled against him.

The man's hand dropped to his side and he stepped towards the minibus.

'*Inglês?*' he said, looking into the minibus at Jase and Marie.

Jase said nothing and stared straight ahead at the windscreen. Marie didn't move. The driver flicked his cigarette butt into the bushes, leant out of the open window and said something. The man ignored him.

'*Inglês?*' he repeated, his head inside the minibus.

The driver spoke again, sharply this time, but the man continued.

'*Inglaterra?*' he shouted and Jase flinched, but didn't respond. The driver was angry now, he yelled something and the man checked his watch and swore.

'English,' a woman said from the back of the bus, 'he ask if you English.'

Jase half-turned to her and then looked up into the man's dark eyes.

'English, yes,' he said. 'We're English.'

The man stared at him for a moment, grunted and stepped away from the minibus.

'*Todos sair!*' he said and the passengers started getting out. The kid that had been yelling destinations stood watching in silence.

Marie turned to Jase.

'What now?'

He slipped the camera into her bag.

'We'd better get out.'

The woman next to them was struggling with the heavy bundle under the seat, so Jase gave a hand. By the time he'd helped her to carry it over to the huddled passengers, the bus had emptied and only Marie and the driver were left inside. Jase looked around, saw the dark shape of the man watching, tall and broad, hands deep in the pockets of his baggy joggers. He went back to help Marie, heard movement behind him and was knocked forward in a blur of pain.

CHAPTER SEVEN

A block away from the security gates and high fences of Copacabana's plush residential district, the car slowed at the approach to a steep road hemmed in by shabby concrete walls.

'Where are we?' asked Simon.

'The back entrance to Santa Marta favela,' John replied.

'Is that one of the safe ones?'

'No.'

Simon ran his hand through his hair.

'Why the back entrance?' he asked.

'It's more discreet.'

The driver braked and left the engine to idle. Five or six figures in scruffy vests and shorts moved away from the wall and into the headlights, armed and watchful. One approached the car cradling a battered assault rifle, finger on the trigger and barrel pointed at the night sky.

'He can't be more than fourteen,' Simon murmured.

John didn't answer, but kept an eye on the kid as he slouched up to the driver's window and gave the glass a sharp rap with his thumb ring. The driver turned his head to John and raised an eyebrow.

John nodded. 'Open it.'

The window slid down and the kid brought the gun to his shoulder, closed one eye and targeted the driver in his sights. Keeping both hands on the steering wheel and speaking in a level voice, the driver asked for permission to enter.

'Yeah, if you give me a ride up.'

Without waiting for an answer, the kid walked around to the passenger side, pulled on the door handle and banged on the window when he found it locked.

'No!' John shouted in Portuguese. 'No guns in the car.'

The kid swore, stepped back and aimed at the glass. Simon shrank into his seat and the driver raised his hands, but John leant forward, pressed a button on the centre console and the passenger window opened. He addressed the kid again.

'We're here to see the Mother of the Gods, she'll be angry if she hears you've kept us waiting.'

The kid sniffed, wiped his nose with the back of his hand and squinted down the gun barrel at John.

'He's coked up to the eyeballs,' John muttered to Simon, and then switched back to Portuguese:

'We're already late, let's go.'

'Give me a ride up.'

'No guns in the car.'

Another sniff. The kid glared at them and then looked away. He shouted something to the others and one of them yelled back. His shoulders slackened, he loosened his grip on the rifle and lashed a sullen kick at the car tyre.

'Get the fuck out of here!'

The driver gunned the engine and a volley of loose stones ricocheted off the chassis as the wheels spun and the car lurched up the hill.

Simon sat back in his seat and turned to John.

'Who on earth is the Mother of the Gods?' he asked.

CHAPTER EIGHT

Marie was trapped. The man was outside, blocking the doorway, and the driver had turned in his seat to face her, cigarette smouldering at the corner of his mouth. Jase lay half inside the minibus, face down in the aisle. She knelt and touched his shoulder, began to panic, but resisted, took a breath, held it and released it.

'Babe, are you OK? Can you hear me?'

Nothing.

The man slapped her hand away, grabbed Jase by the back of his shirt and shoved him further inside. He stepped in, bent over him and when Marie saw something shining in his hand the adrenalin burst out of her in a rage.

'Leave him alone!'

She lunged at him with the nail file, tearing a gash in his shoulder that drew a bellow of fury. She stabbed him again, dimly aware that he was shifting to face her, but sensed little more than the rhythmic rise and fall of her arm until he stunned her with a punch to the head.

Dazed and nauseous, she watched him hunch over Jase and heard the tinny clanking of metal on metal that intensified when Jase groaned, shook his arm and cried out with pain. She groped around for the nail file, found her bag instead, pulled out the camera and hurled it at the man's head, but it missed and clattered to the minibus floor.

He swore and slung it outside then seized her by the arm and she struggled, kicked and scratched.

'Get out Jase!' she screamed, 'Get out now!'

'I can't!' he cried and she went limp with shock when she saw him. He was lying in the aisle on his side and his arm, twisted awkwardly across his face, was handcuffed to the leg of a seat.

The man dragged her off the minibus, slammed the sliding door and ran to the passenger side as the driver crunched the engine into gear.

'Jase!'

She jumped at the running board, gripped the door handle and tugged, but it wouldn't give. She tried again, felt it shift beneath her and when the driver accelerated hard it slid back along the side of the bus with her clinging on.

'Come on, Jase!' she shouted. 'Do something!'

He grabbed at the open door with his free hand, pulled at the handcuffs and cried out in pain.

'I can't!'

She saw his arm jerk and he cried out again.

'I can't!'

'No! Jase, please! You can!'

They were on a straight and the minibus was picking up speed. Squinting into the rushing night, her body flattened against the door, she saw the trunks of huge palms racing by, the long shadows thrown by stones on the dirt track and she saw the driver leering at her in the wing mirror, a cigarette still glowing in his mouth. He turned back to the road, stamped hard on the brake and she hurtled forward as the door slammed shut, lost her grip and flew through the humid air, heard Jase scream her name and blacked out before she hit the ground.

Freya Wolfe lives and works in the Peak District. She is the recipient of the 2018 David Higham Scholarship for Crime Fiction. Juggling a teaching career with raising three children, dogs and some poultry, she has made her career around words, just like the protagonist of her first novel.

criminalcapers@gmail.com
www.freyawolfe.com

Between the Lines

It was the worst of February weather as DI Gabriel Slater strode hard up the hill towards the furtive activity ahead of him. Only just past nine in the morning but he could already tell that this was a day that was never going to see daylight, with rain that was too spiteful to hustle up and snow properly. The kind of invasive dampness that got inside the bones and made it feel like he'd never dry out sank through his raincoat. Even the street lights were uncertain about whether it was day or night, half of them flickering on and off. There'd seemed little point bothering with an umbrella in the face of such meteorological malevolence.

He flashed his credentials to a young officer stood manning the crime scene tape and then ducked under. The officer handed him a package of an unopened protective body suit and carefully entered his details on the scene log.

'Stick this somewhere,' Slater said, shrugging off his raincoat and handing it to the PC. He hauled on the white oversuit and yanked flattering booties over his shoes, casting his eye over the scene around him. He knew that the photographer would already have taken shots in the round of the whole area, but the flat light of a picture didn't tell him nearly as much about the scene as just looking at it did. The cordon marked off one end of an alleyway, cornered on one side by a bar, and the other by a vintage clothes shop. Opposite stood the great and good of Sheffield's nightlife, the Wetherspoon's, in the old Waterworks building, sitting uncomfortably next to the grand City Hall. It was fairly well patrolled by uniformed officers and PCSOs because of the proliferation of bars, pubs and clubs and he wondered how a murder could have happened in such a visible area, even if it were later at night.

'Handy location,' offered his sergeant, Mark Dawson, as Slater approached.

'Nice to have a bit of fresh air on a morning,' grumbled Slater. The scene was just a ten-minute walk away from their base on Snig Hill; in truth, he'd have preferred something a bit further out so that he could have justified his car and the heating.

'What've we got?'

'Body found by the bar staff coming to open up this morning at 7a.m.' Dawson nodded to the bar on the corner.

'Bar opening at seven?'

'Diversification, boss. Can't just be a bar any more. Got to offer brunches and afternoon teas.'

The alley was tight, too narrow even to fit a car down, and black plastic bags were heaped up on either side. The furthest edge was marked by more crime scene tape, a burly officer preventing anyone from entering at that end. Slater pulled the hood of the suit up around his head, stopping the water dripping down his neck, and stepped gingerly around an accumulation of muddy puddles. Activity was on the right, scene-of-crime officers already busy swabbing and taking relevant samples.

He surveyed carefully, trying to be scientific in his gaze, avoiding the emotions that always swirled when he was met with such horror. The body of a young woman arched backwards over a pile of rubbish, her positioning almost graceful despite the hideous surroundings. She looked like a black and white movie star in the shadows of the February alley, her skin grey, hair pale. A barrier tent had been erected quickly above her, but the rain had already slicked her skin, moisture catching the light as he moved towards her and creating the illusion of life. The none-too-nice aroma of urine hung in the air and Slater didn't like to contemplate the number of late night drinkers who might have been caught short in the alley.

'Any idea who she is?' Slater asked, turning to Dawson.

Dawson shook his head. 'Not yet. No sign of any ID or purse or anything. SOCOs reckon she used to have a watch on, but it's not clear whether it's been nicked or not.'

'Sexual assault?' Slater hoped not but was fearful.

'Impossible to say yet. She's not wearing knickers. Again, could be a lifestyle choice rather than they've been removed.'

Slater nodded and stepped carefully closer to the body. Activity around them stopped momentarily as he studied the poor girl whose life had ended in such a horrible way. He thought she'd probably been beautiful but it was impossible to tell now. Beauty for him was about spirit and life, and this poor lass had neither of those any more. Blonde hair, stained rusty red in places, haloed around her head. Her face was turned towards the wall, the angle pulling open the garish wound on her neck. She was wearing a short, silver-sequinned dress that was ruched up around her waist, revealing long legs. A black blazer was lying under her shoulders. A large pool of blood spread out from beneath the plastic bags, saturating the ground below. From what he could see, in addition to the gaping neck, the body was covered with what looked like shallow slashes, punctuated by deeper stab wounds. He'd seen some truly horrible scenes in the past, particularly when he was in uniform and had had to attend a massive pile-up on the M1, but there was something especially unnerving about such deliberate death.

'Divisional surgeon been?' He directed the question towards Dawson without wanting to look away from the scene. It was important to him that he faced it head-on, noticed everything he could, from the way she was positioned to what she was lying on through to the smells around them.

'Yep. Confirmed death.'

'Give us a rough idea of cause?'

Dawson consulted his notebook. 'Wouldn't give much away. Did say that the slash to the neck was ante-mortem and was possible cause of death. Reckoned the rest of the wounds could be window dressing. He wouldn't commit on the possibility of sexual assault either.'

'Time of death?'

'Again, we've got to wait for the postmortem but he reckoned sometime after midnight and before two this morning based on temperature. Said they can do some more tests later to close it down a bit.'

'Any weapon?' Slater knew he was firing questions at Dawson but wanted to make sure he didn't miss anything in this first swoop. The quicker he got the information, the quicker they could assign tasks and work out their approach.

'Not found yet. Still got a whole lot more to sift through.'

Slater studied the body a little more, eyes desperately searching for anything else that might help the victim, a clue to her identification or what had brought her here.

'Here, Bitch-in-Charge,' Dawson hissed, urgently.

Slater stood up and turned to face the alley entrance, frowning at the sergeant. The name was apt, but he disliked its use. For some reason, he had the urge to salute every time his DCI came near. There was something about Zahra Hussain that inspired fear. Perhaps it was the ruthless ambition that obviously accompanied someone who'd made DCI before 35, despite being female and Muslim. That or the hard stare and sharp tone that made even the most experienced copper quake. She was an inspiring woman.

'What have we got?' she barked, before she even made it within ten feet of him. Her face was fierce, framed neatly by the white coverall she'd donned.

Slater filled her in quickly.

'Hmm,' she said, sounding suspicious that they were failing her already. She stepped forward and surveyed the scene. 'I want details. Update in my office as soon as you get back.' She spun round to face him, nodded and then away, back ramrod straight. The officer on the tape went up on tiptoe to lift it over her head so she barely broke stride as she moved under.

'Thanks for the royal visit,' muttered Dawson. Slater simply shook his head, staring after her. He was never entirely sure that she didn't have extraterrestrial hearing and was particularly careful not to say anything that could be misconstrued. She was unusual in even attending the scene. Most bosses in his experience preferred to stay well behind the desk, but she still liked to keep her nose in. It made reporting to her much easier; he admired the way she contributed her own ideas, probing his mind to tease out solutions.

Slater caught the eye of the Crime Scene Manager and stopped quickly for an update.

'Blood spatter analysis could give us some interesting data. This is obviously the kill site and spatter over there,' the CSM pointed to the wall opposite the body, 'might tell us something about the weapon and the assailant or assailants. There's going to be loads of contributory DNA here so we're just swabbing everything we think might be pertinent. Lots of loose items to take and sift through. It's a volume job really. We've set the cordon fairly tight but even then, masses of potential evidence.'

'Tony!' The CSM and Slater turned their heads towards the shout. A SOCO in anonymous white came towards them, waving a silver bag. 'Tony, sir,' she said, addressing the pair in turn as she approached. 'Just found this underneath those rubbish bags over there.' She gestured with her hand.

'Open it,' Tony instructed. Gingerly, she unzipped it.

'Some money, looks like about hundred quid in twenties. Lipstick. Mac, nice. Couple of condoms. Some paracetamol. And this.' She pulled out a driver's licence and presented it with a flourish.

A low whistle behind him alerted him to Dawson's presence.

'Do you know her?' Slater asked his sergeant, over his shoulder.

'You mean you don't?' Dawson replied, rolling his eyes.

'Kitty Wakelin,' contributed Tony, reading the licence. 'Bugger me.' He nodded sagely.

'Who is she?' Slater asked, annoyed.

'Singer? Just nominated for a Brit Award for Best Newcomer? Sheffield's best apparently.'

Slater shrugged. It still didn't mean anything to him. He wasn't keen on music full stop. All those passions and emotions just left him feeling slightly disorientated.

'If she's so famous, why didn't you recognise her?' he asked, pointedly.

'Well, you know... I didn't really look. She was all bloody and facing the wall and stuff. Couldn't really see her,' replied Dawson, sheepishly.

'Right, well, we'll be having a slightly more definite ID before notifying the media I think,' he replied, dryly.

'It's her.' Dawson was confident and bizarrely jovial. 'And you know what that means? Career make or break.'

'Thanks. We'll leave you to it and co-ordinate when you know a bit more about what there might be,' he said to Tony, who nodded to the SOCO. She strode off to bag and tag the evidence. 'Right then,' Slater said, turning towards Dawson, 'let's have a quick chat with our barman.'

Dawson looked to his notes again. 'Name's Steven Morris. He's back inside the bar, Grey's. Left a PC with him.' Slater and Dawson pulled off their coveralls as they entered the bar, stamping their feet automatically as though snow had accumulated on their boots. They handed them to a convenient SOCO who added them to an ever-increasing load.

Grey's, the bar on the corner, was clearly aiming to be an upmarket choice, dark grey paint fresh on the woodwork, windows large and clean. Inside, Slater took in a well-polished oak floor and light coloured walls. The decor was quirky, stuffed squirrels running up the wall, artfully placed bookshelves and uplighters. Split-level, there were a variety of different table styles and sizes scattered around the room. He preferred his furniture to match neatly, but he knew this kind of untidy heap of mismatched old tat was very popular with those in the know these days. Picking up a menu, Slater noted the expensive wine list and extensive cocktail options. Despite that, it still felt a little seedy in the daylight, like so many pubs that were just never designed to be seen in natural light.

At a small table in one of the large fronting windows sat a man of around thirty. A dark fringe hung in his face, his head bowed low as he nursed what looked like a mug of hot tea. Standing a couple of metres away, a young Asian officer watched him a little nervously.

'Mr Morris?' The witness's head jerked up and his eyes met Slater's. Dark stubble shaded his chin; he gave a curt nod. 'Thanks for waiting. I'm sorry to keep you here. I'm sure you'd like to go home.'

'S'all right,' Morris replied with a shrug. He looked fairly pale, but Slater wasn't sure if he was naturally pasty or it was the result of the shock.

'Do you mind just going over with me what happened?' Slater pulled a wooden seat out and sat down opposite him. Behind, Dawson tapped his pen open, ready to note down anything salient.

'You mean, like what?' Morris asked. He didn't sound local, more South in his accent than Yorkshire. 'I found her. Found her like that!'

Slater recognised the defensive tone in his voice. It could be nothing. So many people were automatically defensive whenever they spoke to the police, like all their deepest secrets were about to be ferreted out.

'I mean, take me through your morning,' Slater said. 'What time did you get here? What did you do? That kind of stuff.'

'I got here about 6.30. Bar closes at two and there's always a load to do before we open at nine,' Morris offered, leaning back in his chair. He tossed his head lightly to the side, shifting the fringe out of what were surprisingly feminine brown eyes.

'How do you get to work? Bus? Car?'

'Just walked. I only live up at Park Hill,' he said, naming a local development of apartments. Good central location, pretty pricey though.

'So you come from the south side? Didn't walk past the alley on your way in?' Slater asked, gesturing to the window.

Morris turned his head as though to check himself. 'Nah, came from the other direction. Unlocked the door and came straight in here. Cleaners did the floor last night so I started by taking the chairs down. About seven I went to take the rubbish out. That's when I found her.' He went even paler suddenly, as though remembering the sight that had greeted him. He took a swig of his tea and Slater gave him a moment.

He leaned forward. 'Did you touch her?'

'No,' Morris started, panicked. 'I didn't... I couldn't. It was horrible. I just left her there and came and phoned for an ambulance. Was that right?' he asked, his face horrified. 'Was she... I mean, could I...?'

'She was probably already dead. You did the right thing. Not much anyone can hope to do when faced with something like that.' Slater paused. 'Mr Morris, when you saw her, did you think she looked familiar? Any chance you'd seen her before?'

The barman thought for a few minutes, his eyes fixed on a point above Slater's head. 'No. I mean... I couldn't really see her face or anything. There's a lamp post at the end but it hardly lights the alley and I didn't, you know, stop and stare or anything. She just looked like any other girl.'

Slater nodded. 'Did you notice anything else unusual this morning? See anything out of place? Anyone weird hanging around?' *Anyone with a big sign saying I did it*, he added in his head.

'No,' he replied. 'All as normal as.'

'Did you work last night?'

'No, I just do day shifts,' Morris replied.

'Right then, can you give PC Mahtani here a list of all the staff who worked last night's shift?'

Morris nodded eagerly, pleased to be able to contribute something. 'Do you have any cameras on the property, Mr Morris?'

'Sure. One covers the entrance outside and then we've got one on the bar and two covering the rest of the space,' he pointed them out as he spoke.

'Great, do you think you can get the film from last night sent over?'

'Dunno. I mean, I don't see why not but I'll have to ask the boss.'

'If you give his name to the PC here, we can ask him that too,' Slater replied. He didn't really want a middleman in the way and would be able to impress the urgency on Morris's boss.

'Do you think we'll be able to open tonight? Boss will be wondering,' asked the barman, reluctantly.

Whether he was enquiring out of sensitivity for the victim or because he wanted the day off, Slater wasn't sure. 'I don't think so. Until Scene of Crime have finished processing the alleyway, we'll have to insist you remain closed.'

Dr Vida Henrikson looked out across the audience and tried a smile. 'As police officers, you're aware of the importance of the words we use.' Her throat felt dry and she couldn't hide the flush in her cheeks. No matter how many times she lectured, talking to an audience of professionals always terrified her. A victim of permanent, self-imposed imposter syndrome.

'Making sure the PACE warning is given correctly. Using the right words in an interview situation to retrieve the information you need without being accused of coercion. Selecting the best way to communicate with a witness, a suspect, or a grieving family member. You're aware of the importance of the words *you* use.'

At least this group looked a lot more interested than her undergraduates. Before she'd started lecturing, she'd assumed that the modern student was eagle-eyed and beaver-keen due to the hefty tuition fees they forked over. Instead she regularly encountered the same bleary-eyed and less-than-polite yawning that had been rife when she was a student. Still, to give them their dues, when she'd yawned it had usually been the result of late-night shots in the uni bar; for the modern student, it was more likely to be from the three jobs they were working outside of their degree to try and make ends meet.

'But think about how much can be gained by examining the words that aren't deliberately chosen. The words that unconsciously reveal so much about you. Every place you've lived, everyone you've communicated with, even what you've watched on television, can have an impact on the shape of your speech. Just by listening to a voice we can find out about where that person has been, what experiences have shaped their lives. I want you to think about your own language right now. Where does your language come from and what would we be able to deduce about you, do you think?'

She took advantage of the rhetorical question to have a break, gulping a glass of water, very aware of the fact that she was racing through her presentation. She was booked for the hour; she needed to make sure she wasn't left with empty airtime for the last fifteen minutes of it. Speaking to around thirty police officers today, her lecture formed part of the South Yorkshire Police Professional Education Scheme that was aiming to equip its officers with the tools and skills needed for modern policing. The force seemed to be desperately trying to improve their reputation after the last few years of shameful historical debacles with the Hillsborough and Orgreave Enquiries. These were the newest recruits to start working in CID, an eclectic mix of gender, age and race that represented the face of a much more accessible and forward-thinking police force. As professionally junior as they were, this didn't help with her nerves. She tucked strands of a blonde bob behind her ear once more and then took another deep breath.

'And it's not just our spoken language. The same variances that can distinguish a Geordie's oral utterances from that of a Londoner can be used to examine the written word. And if you just stop for a minute and think about all the utterances we make during the day, whether oral or written, then you can begin to see the potential for this science in helping you to identify criminals and achieve convictions. Suicide notes, ransom demands, hate mail, abusive tweets and written confessions can all be linguistically analysed to help determine authorship. And they're just the obvious forensic texts. Think about the possibilities that are open to us if we consider all the routine communication that occurs and how we can use that in pursuit of justice. The possibilities really are endless.'

She flicked the slideshow behind her on to the picture of a young woman, pretty in an average kind of way, a big smile across her face. The audience shuffled upwards, their backs all a bit straighter. Everyone found the real, practical case studies more interesting than the theoretical. Human nature, she supposed, to want to gawk at the reality, no matter how horrible it was if you stopped to think about it.

'I'm going to tell you a story now. The story of a young bride, her handsome husband and how it all went wrong. How our young bride disappeared and how forensic linguistics helped to solve the case. Her story.' She indicated the projected image. Finally, in the hands of the victims, her nerves settled and she took them through one of the first cases she'd worked on at the university.

'Thank you.' She nodded her head, glad it was over, and walked off the stage quickly to a smattering of applause. The shuffling in seats and stretching started before she'd even left the room. The Q&A had gone relatively smoothly. There was always one fervent detractor who argued that forensic linguistics would be as much use to them in finding criminals as asking a fairy godmother for help. She didn't think it was sexist to note that 90% of the time said detractor was male and the vocal commentator here had been no different. Young, cocky, thought he knew it all, he'd peppered her with questions about the validity of the data and the realistic potential of an actual crime-solving solution, while treating her responses to teenager-worthy eye rolls. Thankfully, everyone else seemed pretty open to what she had talked about and she had the practical cases to back the research up. The detractor had soon been shouted down and she wondered how long he'd represent that modern face of policing.

'Good job, Vida,' her supervisor, George, greeted her with his booming voice. 'Just caught the tail end and it seemed to be as powerful as ever. I'm telling the Vice-Chancellor great things about you and the work you're doing with the police at the minute. Covering yourself, and the university with glory. Exactly what the powers that be enjoy.'

Vida smiled wryly. Despite only being a recent addition to the academic team, she already hated the politics of the job, but knew that if she played the academia game then they left her alone to pursue her particular interests in the field. She'd been lucky in being able to push for Forensic Linguistics even to make it into the modules they offered. Straddling the arts and the sciences gave her double coverage in course delivery though and bringing in finance from the local police force was an extra feather in her cap.

'So, actually, Vida, I'm glad I caught you,' George continued. 'Got a little proposal for you. Some friends of the Vice-Chancellor have got themselves a bit of a situation and we were wondering whether you'd be able to help them out.'

Inwardly, Vida groaned. A bit of a situation didn't sound like the kind of task that would further her scientific research. 'I am quite busy at the minute, George,' she said, 'you know, it's dissertation time of year.'

'Oh, I know Vida. I know. And I wouldn't ask if I didn't think it was important. Mr and Mrs Donaldson are big university donors. He owns Spintech,' he said, naming one of Sheffield's biggest technology companies, 'and they've always given very generously.'

'Right,' said Vida, pursing her lips and squashing a sigh.

'It's not just the money though. In fact, it's not the money at all here. I'd really like it if you could just hear them out and decide whether you could help or not. If not, it's fine, no pressure. Mr Donaldson was really adamant that he wanted it made clear that this is not a task he's forcing you to do.'

'OK,' agreed Vida. 'When do I meet them?'

George looked uncomfortable. 'Erm, now? I'm sorry,' he said, holding his hands up as though to pacify her. 'But they wouldn't wait. Said they couldn't wait. I checked your diary and you've nothing until a 3pm tutorial. Plenty of time.'

'And this is a task I'm not obligated to do? But they're waiting in your office?' George looked even more uncomfortable. 'Fine,' she agreed with a sigh. 'Just let me go to the bathroom.' He nodded and scurried off as Vida headed towards the bathroom and then the stairs to make the climb to the Linguistics floor, her daily concession to getting fit.

A couple were sat huddled together along one side of a small meeting table. They seemed nothing like the wealthy donors that she'd met in the past, perfectly polished and well groomed. These two looked shabby. Both had red-rimmed eyes and while Mrs Donaldson's hair was obviously expensively coloured, it barely looked brushed. Mr Donaldson looked slightly more together, but there was a slight disarray about his suit, the tie not quite aligned, a smudge of dirt on his shirt collar. George was bustling around a capsule coffee machine in the corner, that whirred and clunked as it distributed an array of coffee styles. He introduced Vida to the Donaldsons, smoothing over the faux pas as Jane Donaldson firmly corrected her title to Doctor. Handing Vida's flat white to her, George sat down on the last available chair, his smile uncomfortably at odds with the atmosphere in the room.

'Now, where were we?' he asked, looking around at them. 'Peter, do you want to explain a little more to Dr Henrikson about your problem.'

'Yes, please,' Peter said, smoothly mannered despite his and his wife's obvious distress. 'It's about our daughter, Maggie. She died in May of last year. They've just held the inquest and they recorded a verdict of suicide.'

'But it wasn't!' burst in Jane, suddenly, her voice harsh. 'It wasn't. She couldn't. She just wouldn't have killed herself.'

Peter lay a comforting hand on his wife's knee and she subsided, retreating physically, cowering into her chair. 'Jane and I both feel that the verdict was a mistake. We can't believe that Maggie killed herself. She had absolutely everything she ever wanted. Her whole life was in front of her. She was bright and beautiful and...' He took a shuddering breath. 'I'm sorry. We just still find it so hard. And we thought the police investigation and inquest would give us answers but instead we have more questions than ever before. We just can't accept it.'

'I'm so terribly sorry for your loss,' Vida said, 'but I'm not quite sure where I come into this?'

'It's the note,' he said. 'Maggie supposedly left a letter. But it was typed and only her name was signed. Is that normal? We don't understand why she typed the letter. Don't people take the time to handwrite their suicide notes?'

'Not always. Not now, when more and more of our communication has been moved online and onto computers. I bet that virtually all your communication is online these days,' Vida said, nodding towards Peter.

'Well, yes. But surely a suicide note is different? Anyway, it's not just that it was typed. We don't think it sounds like Maggie, and we were having dinner with Philip, Dr Lacewing,' he said, naming the university's Vice-Chancellor, 'and he mentioned that he'd got this Forensic Linguistic whizz who was working with the police and specialised in authorship matters.

He said that you'd worked on suicide notes before and could tell whether or not the person who is supposed to have written them did write them.'

Vida sipped her flat white and then wondered whether it would be social suicide to use her finger to get the froth out. Shrugging, she opted for partial humiliation and used the teaspoon to scoop it up. 'I think Dr Lacewing may have been a little kind with that introduction,' she said gently, swallowing her mouthful of foam. 'I have worked as part of a team in the US for a few weeks looking at suicide letters but I would by no means call myself an expert. And the science itself is inexact. We can draw some conclusions by comparing different writing styles but they are by no means definitive ones. The science is at its best with volume texts, where we can really build up a body of style markers. It's difficult with a single letter.'

The Donaldsons' faces dropped even further and Vida felt like she'd just stamped on their puppy.

'Is there nothing you can do?' Peter asked, desperation lacing his voice.

Vida sighed. She sent pleading eyes towards George, hoping that he could extract her from this situation but he was scrupulously avoiding her gaze. This wasn't going to go well. 'I can take a look for you,' she finally conceded, 'and presuming you've got other texts that Maggie wrote, I can compare them to see if there are any recognisable markers of Maggie's style in the suicide letter. But I can't promise I will find anything and I also can't promise that I will find something that suggests Maggie's suicide note wasn't written by her. All I can do is look at what the evidence tells me.'

Peter leaned forward eagerly. 'That's all we want, Dr Henrikson. That's all we want. Just take a look, please.'

Afterword

Endings are the hardest things to get right. On the Creative Writing MA Crime Fiction we spend much time on beginnings, on plotting and planning, fine tuning characterisation, working on tone and voice, setting and period, and of course and in particular menace and motivation. The crime novel is a dynamic beast, no more so than now. At UEA we champion difference, the pushing of boundaries, experimentation and excellence.

At the end of this volume – the second such anthology from graduating MA Crime Fiction students – I believe these ideas and ambitions have been well and truly met. Introduced by Ian Rankin and Laura Joyce, we have been taken on journeys both light and dark, across time and space, with integrity and rigour, insightfulness and humour. Always, however, we have been aware of not just talent and potential, but craft. The crime novel – in whatever current manifestation or sub-genre – is determined in part by technique, resource and structure.

John Le Carré said that the best place to start a novel was as close to the ending as possible. The meaning of this, in relation to a form that is so reliant on narrative drive, pace, suspense, and purpose, is clear. But what makes a good ending? How do you really know when you've got there? David Lodge in *The Art of Fiction* said that novels, if they wanted to be somehow realistic, should perhaps go on and on. They should not end. He also implied that endings were the most difficult of fictional constructs and rarely very successful.

Raymond Chandler, meanwhile, said that he wasn't concerned with endings at all. That his books would function just as well if the last chapter were missing. He also said that he wasn't especially concerned with plot, that his work was determined by characterisation, setting, description and the prose. The words were the thing for Chandler, and bringing life to the page. (And not least putting crime back on the streets.) However, his novels, particularly the first two or three, were artfully constructed, with endings that were neither too soon, or not soon enough.

While their time at UEA, on the MA, is over, the journey for these 13 writers, has in many ways just begun. We have here short extracts from now completed manuscripts, each with endings: various, and, I hope you will agree, timely! Which means seeking the finished novel, and enjoying a process that has been deeply considered over a period of two years.

As ever, the future for these former students, writers, and friends, is, bright, exciting, and one that I hope, and expect, will prove to be rewarding. We are all better resourced, and experienced, following such an intensive two years, to create and judge that ending. Even though it might now feel that it's come too soon, and that a slower beginning, might, after all, have something going for it.

Lastly, I want to thank Laura Joyce for the huge part she has played in making the MA such an extraordinarily successful world-class creative critical mix.

Acknowledgements

This anthology comprises extracts from the novels written by the 2018 cohort of UEA's MA in Creative Writing Crime Fiction. The anthology would not have been possible without the generosity of the UEA School of Literature, Drama and Creative Writing in partnership with Egg Box Publishing.

We would like to thank our course directors Henry Sutton and Laura Joyce and tutors Tom Benn and William Ryan for their faith, guidance and support. Thank you also to the 2017 cohort for leading the way, and giving us advice.

Our course has been privileged to have masterclasses from many exciting and inspirational crime authors. Thank you to Ian Rankin, Denise Mina, Julia Crouch, Arne Dahl, Mick Herron and Nicola Upson for sharing their knowledge and experience with us. Thank you also to Professor Mark Wilkinson, Lee Gibbs and the rest of the staff at Norfolk and Norwich University Hospital Mortuary for a fascinating and insightful tour and talk, and to Dr Jack Hartnell for an interesting and inspiring seminar.

A huge thank you to Rachel Hore and Nathan Hamilton for managing the anthologies' publication, Emily Benton for her wonderful book design, and Sarah Gooderson for her extremely thorough proofreading. Thanks to editors Mark Wightman and Roe Lane.

Thanks to Norwich Waffle House and Gonzo's for sustenance and entertainment on our visits to Norwich, and to UEA Broadview Lodge for putting up with us afterwards.

With grateful thanks to all the funders who support the scholarships that support our crime fiction writers, in particular:
   The David Higham Scholarship (Crime Fiction)
   The Main Scholarship

And finally, thanks to our families and friends for their patience and support throughout the course and always.

UEA Creative Writing MA Anthology: Crime writing, 2018

First published by Egg Box Publishing, 2018
Part of UEA Publishing Project Ltd.

A CIP record for this book is available from the British Library.
Printed and bound in the UK by Imprint Digital.

Designed by Emily Benton.
emilybentonbookdesigner.co.uk

Proofread by Sarah Gooderson.
Distributed by NBN International
10 Thornbury Road Plymouth
PL6 7PPT +44 (0)1752 2023102
e.cservs@nbninternational.com

ISBN: 978-1-911343-41-7